PUFFIN BOOKS

RUSTY GOES TO LONDON

For over forty-five years Ruskin Bond has been wriring stories, novellas, essays, poems and children's books. He has written over 500 short stories and articles, many of which have been published by Penguin India.

Ruskin Bond grew up in Jamnagar, Dehradun, New Delhi and Simla. As a young man, he spent four years in the Channel Islands and London. He returned to India in 1955, and has never left the country since. His first novel *The Room on the Roof* received the John Llewellyn Rhys Prize, awarded to a Commonwealth writer under thirty, for 'a work of outstanding literary merit'. He received a Sahitya Akademi Award in 1993, and the Padma Shri in 1999.

He lives in Landour, Mussoorie, with his extended family.

In the same series

Rusty, the Boy from the Hills
Rusty Runs Away
Rusty and the Leopard

RUSTY
Goes to London

Ruskin Bond

Illustrations by
Kallol Majumder

PUFFIN BOOKS

Books Ltd)

Penguin Group (Australia), 250 Camberwell Road, Camberwell, Victoria 3124,
Australia (a division of Pearson Australia Group Pty Ltd)

Penguin Group (NZ), 67 Apollo Drive, Rosedale, Auckland 0632, New Zealand
(a division of Pearson New Zealand Ltd)

Penguin Group (South Africa) (Pty) Ltd, 24 Sturdee Avenue, Rosebank, Johannesburg
2196, South Africa

Penguin Books Ltd, Registered Offices: 80 Strand, London WC2R 0RL, England

First published in Puffin by Penguin Books India 2004

This is a work of fiction. Names, characters, places and incidents are either the
product of the author's imagination or are used fictitiously, and any resemblance to
any actual person, living or dead, events or locales is entirely coincidental.

Typeset in Garamond by SURYA, New Delhi
Printed at Yash Printographics, Noida

PUFFIN BOOKS

PUFFIN BOOKS
Published by the Penguin Group
Penguin Books India Pvt. Ltd, 11 Community Centre, Panchsheel Park,
New Delhi 110 017, India
Penguin Group (USA) Inc., 375 Hudson Street, New York, New York 10014,
USA
Penguin Group (Canada), 90 Eglinton Avenue East, Suite 700, Toronto, Ontario,
M4P 2Y3, Canada (a division of Pearson Penguin Canada Inc.)
Penguin Books Ltd, 80 Strand, London WC2R 0RL, England
Penguin Ireland, 25 St Stephen's Green, Dublin 2, Ireland (a division of Penguin
Books Ltd)
Penguin Group (Australia), 250 Camberwell Road, Camberwell, Victoria 3124,
Australia (a division of Pearson Australia Group Pty Ltd)
Penguin Group (NZ), 67 Apollo Drive, Rosedale, Auckland 0632, New Zealand
(a division of Pearson New Zealand Ltd)
Penguin Group (South Africa) (Pty) Ltd, 24 Sturdee Avenue, Rosebank, Johannesburg
2196, South Africa

Penguin Books Ltd, Registered Offices: 80 Strand, London WC2R 0RL, England
First published in Puffin by Penguin Books India 2004

Copyright © Ruskin Bond 2004

Versions of 'A Far Cry from India', 'Six Pounds of Savings', 'Days of Wine and
Roses' and 'Return to Dehra' appeared in Ruskin Bond's autobiography *Scenes
from a Writer's Life*, as 'A Far Cry from India', 'Three Jobs in Jersey', 'And Another
in London' and 'Return from Dehra' respectively. Pages 14-16 and 19-20 appeared
previously as the short story 'The Typewriter'. A version of 'My Most Important
Day' appeared in *Landour Days: A Writer's Journal*. Pages 229-33 appeared
previously as the short story 'What's Your Dream?'

All rights reserved

14 13 12 11 10 9 8

ISBN 9780143335955

Typeset in *Garamond* by SÜRYA, New Delhi
Printed at Yash Printographics, Noida

Contents

Author's Note

AFTER RETURNING FROM England when I was twenty-one, I have not left the shores of India. I suppose this says something for my attachment to this country, as well as for a secret fear that if I were to go abroad again I would never return. During that lonely year in Jersey, I felt as though I had been banished from India for ever. So I am not taking any chances. Rusty's adventures, as man and writer, will have to continue in India and for his Indian readers. The heart has reasons which reason cannot fathom, and Rusty has always followed the dictates of his heart.

This is the fourth book in the Rusty series, and here we find him in his early twenties, doing his best to become a writer and making a living of it. The early chapters describe his sojourn in Jersey and London, and then we find him back in Dehra Dun, surrounded by 'a handful of nuts', a number of crazy characters who make for some hilarious episodes in the life of the aspiring writer. In 'Shamli' (no resemblance to present-day Shamli), the story is more poignant, its characters trapped in the backwaters of small-town India.

Oddly enough, 'Time Stops at Shamli' was written when I was twenty-one, with the future looking very uncertain. 'A Handful of Nuts' was written when I was sixty-one and not quite the romantic young man of my earlier fiction. But I was beginning to discover that life was really rather funny, provided you did not take yourself too seriously. Although written at an interval of forty years, both stories describe a period in my life that remains fresh and vibrant in my memory.

The concept for the series of Rusty books was Udayan Mitra's. And the credit for bringing continuity and cohesion to the stories goes to Anjana Ramakrishnan, who lives in the little town of Tuticorin in south India—a far cry from London, Shamli and Dehra! She tells me that she is now getting nightmares about Rusty. I don't blame her; I do, too.

But I hope the reader will continue to bear with Rusty. He's no Rambo or James Bond or Harry Potter; just a normal, sensitive youth who is trying to find something bright and meaningful in his life. And along the way he comes across others who are trying to do the same thing.

Landour,   **Ruskin Bond**
Mussoorie   *January 2004*

A Far Cry from India

IT WAS WHILE I was living in Jersey, in the Channel
Islands, that I really missed India.

Jersey was a very pretty island, with wide sandy
bays and rocky inlets, but it was worlds away from
the land in which I had grown up. You did not see an
Indian or Eastern face anywhere. It was not really an
English place either, except in parts of the capital, St
Helier, where some of the business houses, hotels and
law firms were British-owned. The majority of the
population—farmers, fishermen, councillors—spoke a
French *patois* which even a Frenchman would have
disowned. The island, originally French, and then for
a century British, had been briefly occupied by the
Germans. Now it was British again, although it had its
own legislative council and made its own laws. It
exported tomatoes, shrimps and Jersey cows, and
imported people looking for a tax haven.

During the summer months the island was flooded
with English holidaymakers. During the long, cold

winter, gale-force winds swept across the Channel and the island's waterfront had a forlorn look. I knew I did not belong there and I disliked the place intensely. Within days of my arrival I was longing for the languid, easy-going, mango-scented air of small-town India: the gulmohur trees in their fiery summer splendour; barefoot boys riding buffaloes and chewing on sticks of sugarcane; a hoopoe on the grass, bluejays performing aerial acrobatics; a girl's pink dupatta flying in the breeze; the scent of wet earth after the first rain; and most of all my Dehra friends.

So what on earth was I doing on an island, twelve by five miles in size, in the cold seas off Europe? Islands always sound as though they are romantic places, but take my advice, don't live on one—you'll feel deeply frustrated after a week.

I had come here to try my luck at getting my first novel published. There really wasn't much scope for struggling young English authors in India at my time. And I was certainly not going to pursue any other profession.

I had finished school, and then for a couple of years I had been loafing around in Dehra, convinced that my vagrancy in the company of a few friends would give me the right outlook, material and environment to write my first novel.

I'd always wanted to be a writer for nothing made

me happier than being surrounded by books, reading them and then writing. Books had been my sole companions during the many lonely periods of my life. My parents had separated when I was just four and my mother had remarried. I had stayed mostly with Father (wherever his job took us) or with my paternal grandparents in Dehra sometimes. But when I was just eleven, I lost my father to malaria. I stayed for a while with Grandmother, but she too passed away. I was then shunted around for some time—first I stayed with my mother and stepfather, then I was put under the care of my father's cousin Mr John Harrison. I finished my schooling but was at a loose end when circumstances forced me to leave Mr Harrison's house. I became a tutor to Kishen (who was not much younger than me), and lived in a tiny room on the roof of the Kapoors' house, thus making my first serious attempt at defining my own identity.

But life, as usual, had other things in store for me. I was soon without a stable shelter over my head or any means to make a living. I learnt to live each day as it came and to take the tough in my stride. All this only helped to fuel my ambition of becoming a writer someday soon. One day, quite out of the blue, I happened to meet an old acquaintance of my father— Mr Pettigrew, and through him chanced upon a few books left to me by Father.

One of them was a first edition of Lewis Caroll's

Alice in Wonderland. I followed Mr Pettigrew's advice to sell this rare find to a book collector in London. This fetched me a few hundred pounds with which I planned to buy myself a passage to England. Somehow Aunt Emily (my father's cousin) got to know of my future plans and wrote saying that her family (which had settled in Jersey) would be happy to accommodate me with them until I found a job in London. This settled the matter for me, and soon enough I found myself on Ballard Pier and there followed the long sea voyage on the P&O liner, *Strathnaver.* (Built in the 1920s, it had been used as a troopship during the War and was now a passenger liner again.) In the early 1950s, the big passenger ships were still the chief mode of international travel. A leisurely cruise through the Red Sea, with a call at Aden; then through Suez, stopping at Port Said (you had a choice between visiting the pyramids or having a sexual adventure in the port's back alleys); then across the Mediterranean, with a view of Vesuvius (or was it Stromboli?) erupting at night; a look-in at Marseilles, where you could try out your school French and buy naughty postcards; finally docking at Tilbury, on the Thames estuary, just a short train ride away from the heart of London.

At Bombay, waiting for the ship's departure, I had spent two nights in a very seedy hotel on Lamington Road, and probably picked up the hepatitis virus there, although I did not break out in jaundice until I was in Jersey. Bombay never did agree with me. (Now that it has been renamed Mumbai, maybe I'll be luckier.)

I liked Aden. It was unsophisticated. And although I am a lover of trees and forests, there is something about the desert (a natural desert, not a man-made one) that appeals to my solitary instincts. I am not sure that I could take up an abode permanently surrounded by sand, date-palms and camels, but it would be preferable to living in a concrete jungle—or in Jersey, for that matter!

And camels do have character.

Have I told you the story of the camel fair in Rajasthan? Well, there was a brisk sale in camels and the best ones fetched good prices. An elderly dealer was having some difficulty in selling a camel which, like its owner, had seen better days. It was lean, scraggy, half-blind, and moved with such a heavy roll that people were thrown off before they had gone very far.

'Who'll buy your scruffy, lame old camel?' asked a rival dealer. 'Tell me just one advantage it has over other camels.'

The elderly camel owner drew himself up with great dignity and with true Rajput pride, replied: 'There is something to be said for *character*, isn't there?'

Did I have 'character' as a boy? Probably more than I have now. I was prepared to put up with discomfort, frugal meals and even the occasional nine-to-five job provided I could stay up at night in order to complete my book or write a new story. Almost fifty years on, I am still leading a simple life—a good, strong bed, a desk of reasonable proportions, a coat-hanger for my one suit and a comfortable chair by the window. The rest is superstition.

When that ship sailed out of Aden, my ambitions were tempered by the stirrings of hepatitis within my system. That common toilet in the Lamington Road hotel, with its ever-growing uncleared mountain of human excreta, probably had something to do with it. The day after arriving at my uncle's house in Jersey, I went down with jaundice and had to spend two or three weeks in bed. But rest and the right diet brought about a good recovery. And as soon as I was back on my feet, I began looking for a job.

I had only three or four pounds left from my travel money, and I did not like the idea of being totally dependent on my relatives. They were a little disapproving of my writing ambitions. Besides, they were sorry for me in the way one feels sorry for an unfortunate or poor relative—simply because he or she is a relative. They were doing their duty by me, and this was noble of them; but it made me uneasy.

St Helier, the capital town and port of Jersey, was full of solicitors' offices, and I am not sure what prompted me to do the rounds of all of them, asking for a job; I think I was under the impression that solicitors were always in need of clerical assistants. But I had no luck. At twenty, I was too young and inexperienced. One firm offered me the job of tea-boy, but as I never could brew a decent cup of tea, I felt obliged to decline the offer. Finally I ended up working for a pittance in a large grocery store, Le Riche's, where I found myself sitting on a high stool at a high desk (like Herbert Pocket in *Great Expectations*), alongside a row of similarly positioned clerks, making up bills for despatch to the firm's regular clients.

By then it was mid-winter, and I found myself walking to work in the dark (7.30 a.m.) and walking home when it was darker still (6 p.m.)—they gave you long working hours in those days! So I did not get to see much of St Helier except on weekends.

Saturdays were half-holidays. Strolling home via a circuitous route through the old part of the town, I discovered a little cinema which ran reruns of old British comedies. And here, for a couple of bob, I made the acquaintance of performers who had come of age in the era of the music halls, and who brought to their work a broad, farcical humour that appealed to me. At school in Simla, some of them had been familiar through the pages of a favourite comic, *Film Fun*—George Formby, Sidney Howard, Max Miller ('The Cheeky Chappie', known for his double entendres), Tommy Trinder, Old Mother Riley (really a man dressed up as a woman), Laurel and Hardy and many others.

I disliked Le Riche's store. My fellow junior clerk was an egregious fellow who never stopped picking his nose. The senior clerk was interested only in the racing results from England. There were a couple of girls who drooled over the latest pop stars. I don't remember much about this period except that when King George VI died, we observed a minute's silence. Then back to our ledgers.

George VI was a popular monarch, a quiet self-effacing man, and much respected because he had stayed in London through the Blitz when, every night for months, bombs had rained on the city. I thought he deserved more than a minute's silence. In India we observed whole holidays when almost any sort of dignitary or potentate passed away. But here it was 'The King is dead. Long live the Queen!' And then, 'Stop dreaming, Bond. Get on with bills.'

The sea itself was always comforting and on holidays or summer evenings I would walk along the seafront, watching familiar rocks being submerged or exposed, depending on whether the tide was coming in or going out. On Sundays I would occasionally go down to the beach (St Helier's was probably the least attractive of Jersey's beaches, but it was only a short walk from my aunt's house) and sometimes I'd walk out with the tide until I came to a group of prominent rocks, and there I'd sunbathe in solitary and naked splendour. Not since the year of my father's death had I been such a loner.

I could swim a little but I was no Johnny Weissmuller and I took care to wade back to dry land once the tide started turning. Once a couple had been trapped on those rocks; their bodies had been washed ashore the next day. At high tide I loved to watch the sea rushing against the sea wall, sending sprays of salt water into my face. Winter gales were frequent and I liked walking into the wind, just leaning against it. Sometimes it was strong enough to support me and I fell into its arms. It wasn't as much fun with the wind behind you, for then it propelled you along the road in a most undignified fashion, so that you looked like Charlie Chaplin in full flight.

Back in the little attic room which I had to myself, I kept working on my novel, based on the diaries I had kept during my last years in Dehra. It remained a journal but I began to fill in details, trying to capture the sights, sounds and smells of that little corner of India which I had known so well. And I tried to recreate the nature and character of some of my friends—Somi, Ranbir, Kishen—and the essence of that calf-love I'd felt for Kishen's mother. I could have left it as a journal, but in that case it would not have found a publisher. In the 1950s, no publisher would have been interested in the sentimental diaries of an unknown twenty-two-year-old. So it had to be turned into a novel.

Six Pounds of Savings

I WAS FORTUNATE to discover the Jersey Library, and at this time I went through almost everything of Tagore's that had been published in those early Macmillan editions—*The Crescent Moon, The Gardener* and most of the plays—as well as Rumer Godden's Indian novels—*The River, Black Narcissus, Breakfast at the Nickolides.* And there was a Bengali writer, Sudhin Ghosh, who'd written a couple of enchanting memoirs of his childhood in rural Bengal—*And Gazelles Leaping* and *Cradle in the Clouds*; it's hard to find them now.

Jean Renoir's film of *The River* was released in 1952, and as I sat watching it in a St Helier cinema, waves of nostalgia flowed over me. I went to see it about five times. After three months with Le Riche's I found a job as an assistant to a travel agent, a single woman in her mid-thirties, who was opening an office in Jersey for Thomas Cook and Sons, the famous travel agency for whom she had been working in London. She was an efficient woman but jumpy, and she smoked a lot to calm her nerves. Although I abhorred the smoking habit, I was often finding myself in the company of heavy smokers—first my mother and stepfather, and now Miss Fielding.

Miss Fielding did not remove the cigarette from her lips even when she was on the phone to her London office. Her end of the conversation went something like this: 'Puff-puff—A double-room at the Seaview, did you say?—puff, suck—Separate beds or twin beds?—draw, suck, puff—Separate. They've always had separate beds you say. Okay, puff—They're from South Africa?—puff—This hotel has a colour bar. Oh, they're white—puff—white-white or off-white?'

Colour-conscious Jersey did not encourage dark-skinned tourists from the Asian, African or American continents. I don't think Thomas Cook had any policy on this matter, but we were constantly being told by Jersey hotels that they did not take people of 'colour'. Multi-cultural Britain was still some twenty-five years away.

Miss Fielding wasn't bothered by these (to her) trifles. She was having an affair with a man who sold renovated fire extinguishers. But he could not do anything to reduce her smoking. He came to the office on one or two occasions and tried to talk me into investing twenty-five pounds in his business. I'd be part-owner of ten fire extinguishers, he told me. He was quite persuasive, but as my savings did not exceed six pounds at the time, I could not take up his offer. He bought discarded fire extinguishers and put new life into them, he told me. They were as good as new. So was Miss Fielding, after several afternoon sessions in his rooms.

But Thomas Cook weren't happy. For several hours every day I was left in sole charge of the office, taking calls from London and booking people into the island's hotels. I couldn't help but confuse twin beds with double-beds, and was frequently putting elderly couples who hadn't slept together for years into double-beds, while forcibly separating those who couldn't have enough of each other. Miss Fielding did her best to educate me in this matter of beds but I was a slow learner.

Beds could be changed around, but when I booked a group of Brazilian samba dancers into a hotel meant for 'whites only', I was fired. Later I heard that Miss Fielding had been recalled to London. And her gentleman friend ran foul of the local authorities for passing off his re-charged extinguishers under his own brand name.

My next job was a more congenial one. This was in the public health department. Situated near the St Helier docks, it was a twenty-minute walk from my aunt's house—over the brow of a sometimes gale-swept hill, and down to a broad esplanade in the port area. My fellow clerks, all older than me, were a friendly, good-humoured lot, and I was to work under them as a junior clerk for more than a year.

Working at nights in an attic room provided by my aunt, I soon completed my novel. I hadn't been away from India for too long, but I was very homesick, and writing the book helped to take me back to the people and places I had known and loved.

Working in the same office was a sympathetic soul, a senior clerk whose name was Mr Best. He came from good Lancashire stock. His wife and son had predeceased him, and he lived alone in lodgings near the St Helier seafront. As I lived not far away, I would sometimes accompany Mr Best home after work, walking with him along the sea wall, watching the waves hissing along the sandy beaches or crashing against the rocks.

I gathered from some of his remarks that he had an incurable disease, and that he had come to live and work in Jersey in the hope that a sunnier climate would help him to get better. He did not tell me the nature of his illness; but he often spoke about his son, who had been killed in the War, and about the North Country, which was his home. He sensed that we were, in a way, both exiles, our real homes far from this small, rather impersonal island in the Channel.

He had read widely, and sympathized with my ambitions to be a writer. He had tried it once himself, and failed.

'I didn't have the perseverance, lad,' he said. 'I wasn't inventive enough, either. It isn't enough to be able to write well—you have to know how to tell a good story . . . Those who could do both, like Conrad and Stevenson, those are the ones we still read today. The critics keep telling us that Henry James was a master stylist, and so he was, but who reads Henry James?'

Mr Best rather admired my naïve but determined attempt to write a book.

On a Saturday afternoon I was standing in front of a shop, gazing wistfully at a baby portable typewriter on display. It was just what I wanted. My book was nearly finished but I knew I'd have to get it typed before submitting it to a publisher.

'Buying a typewriter, lad?' Mr Best had stopped beside me.

'I wish I could,' I said. 'But it's nineteen pounds and I've only got six pounds saved up. I'll have to hire some old machine.'

'But a good-looking typescript can make a world of difference, lad. Editors are jaded people. If they find a dirty manuscript on the desk, they feel like chucking it in the wastepaper basket—even if it is a masterpiece!'

'There's an old typewriter belonging to my aunt, but it should be in a museum. The letter "b" is missing. She must have used that one a lot—or perhaps it was my uncle. Anyway, when I type my stories on it, I have to go through them again and ink in all the missing "b"s.'

'That won't do, lad. I tell you what, though. Give me your six pounds, and I'll add thirteen pounds to it, and we'll buy the machine. Then you can pay me back out of your wages—a pound every week. How would that suit you?'

I was both surprised and immensely thrilled. I had always thought Mr Best slightly stingy, as he seldom went to cinemas or restaurants. But here he was, offering to advance me the money for a new typewriter.

I accepted his offer and walked down the street in a state of happy euphoria, the gleaming new typewriter in my hand. I sat up late that night, hammering out the first chapter of my book.

It was midsummer then, and by winter end I had paid back six pounds to Mr Best.

I found Jersey cold in the winter. It did not snow but those gales went right through you, and my sports coat (I had no overcoat) did not really keep the cold out.

Still, there was something quite stirring, electrifying about those gales. One evening, feeling moody and dissatisfied, I deliberately went for a walk in the thick of a gale, taking the road along the seafront. The wind howled about me, almost carrying me with it along the promenade; and as it was high tide, the waves came crashing over the sea wall, stinging my face with their cold spray. It was during the walk that I resolved that if I was going to be a writer I would have to leave Jersey and live and work in London come hell or high water.

This resolve was further strengthened when, a few days later, I happened to quarrel with my uncle over an entry I had made in my diary.

Keeping a diary or journal is something that I have done fitfully over the years, and sometimes it is no more than a notebook of ideas and impressions which go into the making of essays or stories. But when I am lonely or troubled it takes the form of a confessional, and this is what it was at the time. My uncle happened to come across it among my books. I don't think he was deliberately prying but he glanced through it and came across a couple of entries in which I had expressed my resentment over the very colonial attitudes that still prevailed in my uncle's family. He was a South Indian Christian, my aunt an Anglo-Indian, and yet they were champions of Empire!

This was their own business, of course, and they had a right to their views—but what I did resent was their criticism of the fact that I had Indian friends who wrote to me quite regularly. They wanted me to forget these ties and be more British in my preferences and attitudes. Their own children had acquired English accents while I still spoke *chi-chi*!

I forget the exact words of my diary entry (I threw it away afterwards); but my uncle was offended and took me to task. I accused him of going through my personal letters and papers. Although things quietened down the next day, I had resolved to make a move.

Luckily for me, it was then that I received a letter from a publisher (the third to whom I had submitted the book) saying that they had liked my story but had some suggestions to make and could I call on them in London.

I had saved about six pounds from my salary, and after giving a week's notice to the public health department, I packed my rather battered suitcase and took the cross-channel ferry to Plymouth. A few hours later I was in London.

The cheapest place to stay was a student's hostel and I spent a few nights in the cheapest one I could find. The day after my arrival I went to the employment exchange and took the first job that was offered. It didn't seem to matter what I did, provided it gave me enough to pay for my board and lodging and left me free to write on holidays and in the evenings.

I was alone and I was lonely but I was not afraid. In fact, London swept me off my feet. The theatres and bookshops exerted their magic on me. And the publishers said they would take my book if only I'd try writing it again.

At twenty-two, I was prepared to rewrite a book a dozen times, so I took a room in Hampstead, and grabbed the first job that came my way. I would have to keep working until I established myself as a writer. At that point I did not know how long this would take, but my life was only just beginning in many senses so I was very happy.

For some time I did not send any money to Mr Best. My wage was modest, and London was expensive, and I wanted to enjoy myself a little. I meant to write to him, explaining the situation, but kept putting it off, telling myself that I would write as soon as I had some money to send him.

Several months passed. I wrote the book a third time, and this time it was accepted and I received a modest advance. I opened an account with Lloyd's, and then, finally, I made out a cheque in the name of Mr Best and mailed it to him with a letter.

But it was never to be cashed. It came back in the

post with my letter, and along with it was a letter from my former employer saying that Mr Best had gone away and left no address. It seemed to me that he had given up his quest for better health, and had gone home to his own part of the country.

And so my debt was never paid.

The typewriter is still with me. I used it for over thirty years, and it is now old and battered. But I will not give it away. It's like a guilty conscience, always beside me, always reminding me to pay my debts in time.

Days of Wine and Roses

LOOKING BACK ON the two years I spent in London, I realize that it must have been the most restless period of my life, judging from the number of lodging houses and residential districts I lived in— Belsize Park, Haverstock Hill, Swiss Cottage, Tooting and a couple of other places whose names I have forgotten. I don't quite know why but I was never long in any one boarding house. And unlike a Graham Greene character, I wasn't trying to escape from sinister pursuers. Unless you could call Nirmala a sinister pursuer.

This good-hearted girl, the sister of an Indian friend, took it into her head that I needed a sister, and fussed over me so much, and followed me about so relentlessly that I was forced to flee my Glenmore Road lodgings and move to south London (Tooting) for a month. I preferred north London because it was more cosmopolitan, with a growing population of Indian, African and continental students. I had, initially, tried living in a students' hostel for a time but the food was awful and there was absolutely no privacy. So I moved into a bedsitter and took my meals at various snack bars and small cafés. There was a nice place near Swiss Cottage where I could have a glass or two of sherry with a light supper, and after this I would walk back to my room and write a few pages of my novel.

My meals were not very substantial and I must have been suffering from some form of malnutrition because my right eye started clouding over and my sight was partially affected. I had to go into hospital for some time. The condition was diagnosed as Eale's Disease, a rare tubercular condition of the eye, and I felt quite thrilled that I could count myself among the 'greats' who had also suffered from this disease in some form or another—Keats, the Bröntes, Stevenson, Katherine Mansfield, Ernest Dowson—and I thought, If only I could write like them, I'd be happy to live with a consumptive eye!

But the disease proved curable (for a time, anyway), and I went back to my job at Photax on Charlotte Street, totting up figures in heavy ledgers. Adding machines were just coming in but my employers were quite happy with their old ledgers—and so was I. I became quite good at adding pounds, shillings and pence, for hours, days, weeks, months on end. And quite contented too, provided I wasn't asked to enter the higher realms of mathematical endeavour. Maths was never my forte, although I kept reminding myself that Lewis Carroll, one of my all-time favourites, also wrote books on mathematics.

This mundane clerical job did not prevent me from pursuing the literary life, although for most of the time it was a solitary pursuit—wandering the streets of London and the East End in search of haunts associated with Dr Johnson, Dickens and his characters, W.W. Jacobs, Jerome K. Jerome, George and Weedon Grossmith; Barrie's Kensington Gardens; Dickens's dockland; Gissing's mean streets; Fleet Street; old music halls; Soho and its Greek and Italian restaurants.

In these latter I could picture the melancholic 1890s poets, especially Ernest Dowson writing love poems to the vivacious waitress who was probably unaware of his presence. For a time I went through my Dowson period—wistful, dreamy, wallowing in a sense of loss and failure. I had even memorized some of his verses, such as these lovely lines:

They are not long, the days of wine and roses:
Out of a misty dream
Our path emerges for a while, then closes
Within a dream.

Poor Dowson, destined to die young and unfulfilled. A minor poet, dismissed as inconsequential by the critics, and yet with us still, a singer of sad but exquisite songs.

A little down the road from my office was the Scala Theatre, and as soon as I had saved enough for a theatre ticket (theatre-going wasn't expensive in those days), I went to see the annual Christmas production of *Peter Pan*, which I'd read as a play when I was going through the works of Barrie in my school library. This production had Margaret Lockwood as Peter. She had been Britain's most popular film star in the forties and she was still pretty and vivacious. I think Captain Hook was played by Donald Wolfit, better known for his portrayal of Svengali.

My colleagues in Photax, though not in the least literary, were a friendly lot. There was my fellow clerk, Ken, who shared his marmite sandwiches with me. There was Maisie of the auburn hair, who was constantly being rung up by her boyfriends. And there was Clarence, who was slightly effeminate and known to frequent the gay bars in Soho. (Except that the term 'gay' hadn't been invented yet.) And there was our head clerk, Mr Smedly, who'd been in the Navy during the War, and was a musical-theatre buff. We would often discuss the latest musicals—*Guys and*

Dolls, *South Pacific*, *Paint Your Wagon*, *Pal Joey*—big musicals which used to run for months, even years.

The window opposite my desk looked out on a huge hoarding, and it was always an event when a new poster went up on it. Weeks before the film was released, there was a poster of Judy Garland in her comeback film, *A Star Is Born*, and I can still remember the publicity headline: 'Judy, the World Is Waiting for Your Sunshine!' And, of course, there was Marilyn Monroe in *Niagara*, with Marilyn looking much bigger than the waterfall, and that fine actor, Joseph Cotten, nowhere in sight.

My heart, though, was not in the Photax office. I had no ambitions to become head clerk or even to learn the intricacies of the business. It was a nine-to-five job, giving me just enough money to live on (six pounds a week, in fact), while I scribbled away all my evenings, working on the second (or was it the third?) draft of my novel.

How I worked at that book! I was always being asked to put things in or take things out. At first the publishers suggested that it needed 'filling out'. When I filled it out, I was told that it was now a little too descriptive and would I prune it a bit? And what started out as a journal and then became a first-person narrative finally ended up in the third person. But the editors only made suggestions; they did not tamper with my language or style. And the 'feel' of the story—my love for India and my friends in particular—was ever present, running through it like a vein of gold.

Much of the publishers' uncertain and contradictory suggestions stemmed from the fact they relied heavily on their readers' recommendations. A 'reader' was a well-known writer or critic who was asked (and paid) to give his opinion on a book. My manuscript was sent to the celebrated literary critic, William Atkins, who said I was a 'born writer' and likened me to Sterne, but also said I should wait a little longer before attempting a novel. Another reader, Leslie Lamb, said he had enjoyed the story but that it would be a gamble to publish it.

Fortunately, Antony Dahl was the sort of publisher who was ready to take a risk with a new, young author, so instead of rejecting the book, he bought an option on it, which meant that he could sit on it for a couple of years until he had made up his mind!

My mentor at this time was Donna Stephen, Dahl's editor and junior partner. She was at least ten years older than me but we became good friends. She invited me to her flat for meals and sometimes accompanied me to the pictures or the theatre. She was tall, auburn-haired and attractive in a sort of angular English way. Donna was fond of me. She could see I was suffering from malnutrition and as she was a good cook (in addition to being a good editor), she shared her very pleasant and wholesome meals with me. There is nothing better than good English food, no matter what the French or Italians or Chinese may say. A lamb chop, a fish nicely fried, cold meat with salad, or shepherd's pie, or even an Irish stew, are infinitely more satisfying than most of the stuff served in continental or Far Eastern restaurants. I suppose it's really a matter of childhood preferences. For, deep down in my heart, I still fancy a kofta curry because koftas were what I enjoyed most in Granny's house. And oh, for one of Miss Kellner's meringues—but no one seems to make them any more.

I really neglected myself during the first year I spent in London. Never much of a cook, I was hard put to fry myself an egg every morning before rushing off to catch the tube for Tottenham Court Road, a journey of about twenty-five minutes. In the lunch break I would stroll across to a snack bar and have the inevitable baked beans-on-toast. There wasn't time for a more substantial meal, even if I could afford it. In the evenings I could indulge myself a little, with a decent meal in a quiet café; but most of the time I existed on snacks. No wonder I ended up with a debilitating disease!

Perhaps the first relaxing period of my London

life was the month I spent in the Hampstead General Hospital, which turned out to be a friendly sort of place.

I was sent there for my Eale's disease, and the treatment consisted of occasional cortisone injections to my right eye. But I was allowed—even recommended—a full diet, supplemented by a bottle of Guinness with my lunch. They felt that I needed a little extra nourishment—wise doctors, those!

The bottle of Guinness made me the envy of the ward, but I made myself popular by sharing the drink with neighbouring patients when the nurses weren't looking. One nurse was a ravishing South American beauty, and half the ward was in love with her.

It was a general ward and one ailing patient named George—a West Indian from Trinidad—felt that he was being singled out for experimentation by the doctors. He set up a commotion whenever he had to be given a rather painful lumbar puncture. I would sit on his bed and try to calm him down, and he became rather dependent on my moral support, insisting on my presence whenever he was being examined or treated.

While I was in hospital, I got in a lot of reading (with one eye), wrote a short story, and received visitors in style. They ranged from my colleagues at Photax, to Donna Stephen, my would-be publisher, to some of my Indian friends in Hampstead, to my latest landlady, a motherly sort who'd lost some of her children in Hitler's persecution of the Jews.

When I left the hospital I was richer by a few pounds, having saved my salary and been treated free on account of the National Health Scheme. The spots had cleared from my eyes and I'd put on some weight, thanks to the lamb chops and Guinness that had constituted my lunch.

Before I left, George, the West Indian, asked me for my home address, but for some strange reason I did not expect to see him again.

Calypso Christmas

MY FIRST CHRISTMAS in London was a lonely one. My small bed-sitting-room near Swiss Cottage was cold and austere, and my landlady disapproved of any sort of revelry. Moreover, I hadn't much money for the theatre or a good restaurant. That first English Christmas was spent sitting in front of a lukewarm gas-fire, eating beans on toast, and drinking cheap sherry. My one consolation was the row of Christmas cards on the mantelpiece—most of them from friends in India.

But the following year I was making more money and living in a bigger, brighter, homelier room. I had almost forgotten about George—my friend from the hospital—until I found him on my doorstep one day. I always wondered how he had tracked me down to my new address, but I never got around to asking him about it. That day, the two of us went to a nearby pub and drank rum. He invited me to a calypso party in Camden Town, and when I arrived I found I was the only 'white' in a gathering of some forty handsome black men and women, all determined to eat, drink and be merry into the early hours of the morning. I fell asleep on a settee halfway through the party. Someone fell asleep on top of me.

I met George occasionally.

George worked for British Railways. He was a ticket-collector at one of the underground stations. He liked his work, and received about ten pounds a week for collecting tickets.

Like thousands of other West Indians, he had come to England because he had been told that jobs were plentiful, that there was a free health scheme and national insurance, and that he could earn anything from ten to twenty pounds a week—far more than he could make in Trinidad or Jamaica. But, while it was true that jobs were to be had in England, it was also true that sections of local labour resented outsiders filling these posts. There were also those, belonging chiefly to the lower middle-classes, who were prone to various prejudices, and though these people were a minority, they were still capable of making themselves felt and heard.

In any case, London is a lonely place, especially for the stranger. And for the happy-go-lucky West Indian, accustomed to sunshine, colour and music, London must be quite baffling.

As though to match the grey-green fogs of winter, Londoners wore sombre colours, greys and browns. The West Indians couldn't understand this. Surely, they reasoned, during a grey season the colours worn should be vivid reds and greens—colours that would defy the curling fog and uncomfortable rain? But Londoners frowned on these gay splashes of colour; to them it all seemed an expression of some sort of barbarism. And then again Londoners had a horror of any sort of loud noise, and a blaring radio could (quite justifiably) bring in scores of protests from neighbouring houses. The West Indians, on the other hand, liked letting off steam; they liked holding parties in their rooms at which there was much singing and shouting. They had always believed that England was their mother country, and so, despite rain, fog, sleet and snow, they were determined to live as they had lived back home in Trinidad. And it is to their credit, and even to the credit of indigenous Londoners, that this is what they succeeded in doing.

A large, stout man, with huge hands and feet, George always had a gentle, kindly expression on his mobile face. Amongst other accomplishments he could play the piano, and as there was an old, rather dilapidated piano in my room, he would often come over in the evenings to run his fat, heavy fingers over the keys, playing tunes that ranged from hymns to jazz pieces. I thought he would be a nice person to spend Christmas with, so I asked him to come and share the pudding my landlady had made, and a bottle of sherry I had procured.

Little did I realize that an invitation to George would be interpreted as an invitation to all of George's friends and relations—in fact, anyone who had known him in Trinidad—but this was the way he looked at it, and at eight o'clock on Christmas Eve, while a chilly wind blew dead leaves down from Hampstead Heath, I saw a veritable army of West Indians marching down Belsize Avenue, with George in the lead.

Bewildered, I opened my door to them; and in streamed George, George's cousins, George's nephews and George's friends. They were all smiling and they all shook hands with me, making complimentary remarks about my room ('Man, that's some piano!' 'Hey, look at that crazy picture!' 'This rocking chair gives me fever!') and took no time at all to feel and make themselves at home. Everyone had brought something along for the party. George had brought several bottles of beer. Eric, a flashy, coffee-coloured youth, had brought cigarettes and more beer. Marian, a buxom woman of thirty-five, who called me 'darling' as soon as we met, and kissed me on the cheeks saying she adored pink cheeks, had brought bacon and eggs. Her daughter Lucy, who was sixteen and in the full

bloom of youth, had brought a gramophone, while the little nephews carried the records. Other friends and familiars had also brought beer; and one enterprising fellow produced a bottle of Jamaican rum.

Then everything began to happen at once.

Lucy put a record on the gramophone, and the strains of *Basin Street Blues* filled the room. At the same time George sat down at the piano to hammer out an accompaniment to the record. His huge hands crushed down on the keys as though he were chopping up chunks of meat. Marian had lit the gas-fire and was busy frying bacon and eggs. Eric was opening beer bottles. In the midst of the noise and confusion I heard a knock on the door—a very timid, hesitant sort of knock—and opening it, found my landlady standing on the threshold.

'Oh, Mr Bond, the neighbours—' she began, and glancing into the room was rendered speechless.

'It's only tonight,' I said. 'They'll all go home after an hour. Remember, it's Christmas!'

She nodded mutely and hurried away down the corridor, pursued by something called *Be Bop A-Lula*. I closed the door and drew all the curtains in an effort to stifle the noise; but everyone was stamping about on the floorboards, and I hoped fervently that the downstairs people had gone to the theatre. George had started playing calypso music, and Eric and Lucy were strutting and stomping in the middle of the room, while the two nephews were improvising on their own. Before I knew what was happening, Marian had taken me in her strong arms and was teaching me to do the calypso. The song playing, I think, was *Banana Boat Song*.

Instead of the party lasting an hour, it lasted three hours. We ate innumerable fried eggs and finished off all the beer. I took turns dancing with Marian, Lucy, and the nephews. There was a peculiar expression they used when excited. 'Fire!' they shouted. I never knew what was supposed to be on fire, or what the exclamation implied, but I too shouted 'Fire!' and somehow it seemed a very sensible thing to shout.

Perhaps their hearts were on fire, I don't know; but for all their excitability and flashiness and brashness they were lovable and sincere friends, and today, when I look back on my two years in London, that Christmas party is the brightest, most vivid memory of all, and the faces of George and Marian, Lucy and Eric, are the faces I remember best.

At midnight someone turned out the light. I was dancing with Lucy at the time, and in the dark she threw her arms around me and kissed me full on the lips. It was the first time I had been kissed by a girl in London, and when I think about it, I am glad that it was Lucy who kissed me.

When they left, they went in a bunch, just as they had come. I stood at the gate and watched them saunter down the dark, empty street. The buses and tubes had stopped running at midnight, and George and his friends would have to walk all the way back to their rooms at Highgate and Golders Green.

After they had gone, the street was suddenly empty and silent, and my own footsteps were the only sounds I could hear. The cold came clutching at me, and I turned up my collar. I looked up at the windows of my house, and at the windows of all the other houses in the street. They were all in darkness. It seemed to me that we were the only ones who had really celebrated Christmas.

The Stolen Daffodils

IT WAS A foggy day in March that found me idling along Baker Street, with my hands in my pockets, a scarf wound round my neck, and two pairs of socks on my feet. I had taken the day off from work. The BBC had commissioned me to give a talk on village life in India, and, ambling along Baker Street in the fog, thinking of my talk, I realized I didn't really know much about village life in India. True, I could remember the smell of cowdung smoke and the scent of jasmine, and the flood-waters lapping at the walls of mud houses, but I didn't know much about village electorates and that sort of thing, and I was on the point of turning back and making my way to India House to get a few facts and figures, when I realized I wasn't on Baker Street any more. Wrapped in thought, I had wandered into Regent's Park. And now I wasn't sure of the way out.

A tall gentleman wearing a long grey cloak was stooping over a flower-bed, and going up to him, I said, 'Excuse me, sir, can you tell me how I get out of here?'

'How did you get in?' he asked me in an impatient voice, and when he turned and faced me, I received a severe shock. He wore a peaked hunting-cap, and in one hand he held a large magnifying-glass. A long, curved pipe hung from his sensuous mouth. He possessed a long steely jaw, and his eyes had a fierce expression—they were bright with the intoxication of some drug.

'Good heavens!' I exclaimed. 'You're Mr Sherlock Holmes!'

'And you, sir,' he replied with a flourish of his cloak, 'are just out of India, on leave from office, and due to give a lecture on the radio.'

'But—but how did you know all that?' I stammered. 'You've never seen me before. I suppose you know my name too?'

'Elementary, my dear Bond. The BBC notepaper in your hand, on which you have been scribbling, reveals your intention to give a talk. Your name is on the envelope which you hold upside down behind it. It is ten o'clock in the morning, and if you were not either on leave or unemployed you would be sitting in an office. The condition of your clothes would indicate that you are not in want of employment; therefore you must have taken the day off.'

'And how do you know I'm from India?' I said, a trifle resentfully.

'Your accent betrays you,' said Holmes with a superior smile.

I was about to turn away and leave him, when he laid a restraining hand on my shoulder.

'Stay a moment,' he said. 'Perhaps you can help me. I'm surprised at Watson. He promised to be here ten minutes ago, but his wife must have kept him at home. Never marry, Bond. Women sap the intellect.'

'In what way can I help you?' I asked, feeling flattered now that the great man had condescended to take me into his confidence.

'Take a look at this,' said Holmes, going down on his knee near the flower-bed. 'Do you notice anything odd?'

'Somebody's been pulling out daffodils,' I said.

'Excellent, Bond! Your powers of observation are as good as Watson's. Now tell me, what else do you see?'

'The ground is a little trampled, that's all.'

'By what?'

'A human foot. And—yes, a dog has been here too, it's been helping to dig up the bulbs!'

'You astonish me, Bond. You are quicker than I thought you were. Now shall I explain what all this is about? You see, for the past week, someone has been stealing daffodils from the park, and the authorities have asked me to deal with the matter. I think we shall catch our culprit this afternoon.'

I was rather disappointed. 'It isn't very dangerous, is it?'

'Ah, my dear Bond, the days are past when Ruritanian princes lost their diamonds, and duchesses their tiaras. There are no longer any Ruritanian princes in existence, and duchesses cannot afford tiaras. The more successful criminals have legalized their activities, and the East End has been cleaned up. And those cretins at Scotland Yard don't even believe in my existence!'

'I'm sorry to hear that,' I said. 'But who do you think is stealing the daffodils?'

'Obviously it is someone who owns a dog. Someone who takes a dog out regularly for a morning walk. That points to a woman. A woman in London is likely to keep a small dog—and judging from the animal's footprints, it must be either a Pekinese or a miniature Pomeranian. What I suggest, Bond, is that we conceal ourselves behind those bushes, and wait for the culprit to come along. She is sure to come again this morning. She has been stealing daffodils for the past week. And stealing daffodils, like smoking opium, becomes a habit.'

Holmes and I crept behind bushes, and settled

down to a long wait. After half an hour our patience was rewarded. A large elderly woman in a green hat came walking stealthily across the grass, followed by a small white Pom on a lead. Holmes had been right! More than ever, I admired his brilliance. We waited until the woman began pulling daffodil plants out of the soil, and then Holmes leapt from the bushes.

'Ah, we have you, madam!' he cried, springing upon her so swiftly that she shrieked and dropped the daffodils. I sprang out after Holmes, but my effort was rewarded by a nip in the leg from the outraged Pomeranian.

Holmes held the woman by the shoulders. I don't know what frightened her more—being caught, or being confronted by that grim-visaged countenance, with its pipe, cloak and hunting-cap.

'Now, madam,' he said firmly, 'why were you stealing daffodils?'

She had begun to weep, and I thought Holmes was going to soften; he always did, when confronted by weeping women.

'I would be obliged, Bond, if you would call the park attendant,' he said to me.

I hurried off towards a greenhouse, and after a brief search found a gardener.

'Stealing daffodils, is she?' he said, running up at the double, a dangerous-looking rake in one hand.

But when we got to the daffodil-bed, I couldn't find the lady anywhere. Nor was Holmes to be seen. I was overcome by doubt and embarrassment. But then I looked at the ground, and saw a number of daffodils scattered about the place.

'Holmes must have taken her to the police,' I said.

'Holmes,' said the gardener. 'Who's Holmes?'

'Sherlock Holmes, of course. The celebrated detective. Haven't you heard of him?'

The gardener looked at me with increasing alarm. 'Sherlock Holmes, eh? And you'll be Dr Watson, I suppose?'

'Well, not exactly,' I said; but before I could explain, the gardener had disappeared.

I found my way out of the Park eventually, feeling that Holmes had let me down a little; then, just as I was crossing Baker Street, I thought I saw him on the opposite curb. He was alone, looking up at a lighted room, and his arm was raised as though he was waving to someone. I thought I heard him shout 'Watson!' But I was not sure. I started to cross the road, but a big red bus came out of the fog in front of me, and I had to wait for it to pass. When the road was clear, I dashed across. But by that time Holmes had gone, and the rooms above were dark.

My Limehouse Adventure

SO THIS WAS Limehouse: quiet, empty back-streets, with the river lapping against the walls of old houses. A brewery. A few warehouses. A boy speeding along the pavement on roller-skates. But was this the real Limehouse? There were no drunken sailors in the streets. There were no Chinese laundry-houses. Shouldn't a Lascar come stumbling out of a dark doorway with a knife in his back? Wasn't it somewhere on this very street that Watson found Holmes in an opium-den run by a heavily-scarred Malay, while above stairs someone screamed and outside there was a splash in the river? Where were Edgar Wallace's sinister Chinese, and where were the characters of W.W. Jacobs?

Limehouse on a Sunday. Neither Chelsea nor Hampstead could have been more tranquil. Of course the pubs would close soon, and then perhaps the West Indian sailors, now sitting quietly in front of the bar, might suddenly come to life and perform calypsos in the street.

I was feeling hungry, since I had walked almost the entire length of Commercial Road, starting from Petticoat Lane where I had found myself handing over five shillings to a street photographer for taking my picture unasked. (An hour later, when I looked at the photograph, it had faded completely.) On Ming Street—a name reminiscent of more exotic times—I was delighted to find several small restaurants with Chinese names. Most of them were empty. At one time you could count the Chinese in Limehouse by the thousands, but now there weren't more than two or three hundred in the area.

I pushed my way through the swing doors of the Nanking Restaurant and looked around. The place was empty. Tables and chairs were painted a bright green, and decorating the walls were coloured pictures of George V, George VI and Elizabeth II. I had never seen such a patriotic display anywhere other than in the East End.

There was nobody in the restaurant, not even a waiter, so I sat down and rattled a salt-cellar in order to attract attention. But, as no one came, I began to wonder if the owner of the place couldn't afford a waiter and did the serving himself, but even he was nowhere to be seen. The room was as quiet as an empty chapel.

I coughed. The sound startled me. I tried whistling,

but it sounded eerie rather than cheerful. I noticed a jug of water standing on a side-board, and feeling thirsty, got up and made for it. As I couldn't find a glass, I drank the water straight from the jug. I was putting it down when an inner door burst open and an excited Chinese rushed out. Without so much as a glance in my direction, he went through the swing doors and stood uncertainly on the pavement, looking in all directions, before coming in again with an anxious distracted expression. Without a word, he returned to the inner room.

Here was a mystery! Limehouse was living up to its reputation. Perplexed but undaunted, I returned to my table, determined to remain in the restaurant until someone took notice of me. The sign-board outside proclaimed that the place was a restaurant; and as the doors were open, I had every right to sit at a table, and wait to be served—or possibly murdered.

Presently I heard a curtain rustle. It was a girl who came out—a little Chinese girl of about eleven, with her hair in a pigtail and green woollen leggings on her feet. Like the man, she paid no attention to me, but began bouncing a rubber ball on the floor. It bounced too high and came towards me, so I caught it and placed it on the table.

'Pass the ball,' said the girl from the middle of the room.

'Come and get it,' I said. 'And can I get anything to eat here?'

'If you like. Pass the ball.'

'Was that your father who came out just now?'

'Yes. Aren't you going to pass the ball?'

'Tell me, does he serve his customers, or do they just go into the kitchen and help themselves?'

'You'll have to wait,' said the girl. 'My mother's having a baby.'

I threw the ball across the table. She caught it neatly, marched out through the swing-doors, and began bouncing the ball on the pavement. As soon as she had gone, I heard a baby crying in the inner room. For about five minutes I sat listening, and then I began to feel foolish. I was about to leave when the Chinese came bustling into the room, his face creased with smiles.

'I am very sorry, sir!' he exclaimed. 'I have made you wait a long time. But the doctor could not arrive in time, and the baby would not wait for the doctor. So my wife and I—we had to manage by ourselves. All is well now, sir. Here is the menu.'

I gazed at him in wonder, while he bubbled over with enthusiasm.

'Your lunch is on the house, sir,' he said. 'Chicken noodles, chow-mien, lobster fuyong, anything you like! We have had six children, but all girls. Now we have a boy!'

I congratulated him, and accepted the offer of lunch. It was a good meal, lovingly prepared. My long wait had been worthwhile, and Limehouse had, after all, come up to expectations. Where else in London could this have happened to me?

The Man Who Was Kipling

I WAS SITTING on a bench in the Indian section of the Victoria and Albert Museum, when a tall, stooping, elderly gentleman sat down beside me. I gave him a quick glance, noting his swarthy features, heavy moustache, and horn-rimmed spectacles. There was something familiar and disturbing about his face and I couldn't resist looking at him again.

I noticed that he was smiling at me.

'Do you recognize me?' he asked in a soft pleasant voice.

'Well, you do seem familiar,' I said. 'Haven't we met somewhere?'

'Perhaps. But if I seem familiar to you, that is at least something. The trouble these days is that people don't *know* me anymore—I'm a familiar, that's all. Just a name standing for a lot of outmoded ideas.'

A little perplexed, I asked, 'What is it you do?'

'I wrote books once. Poems and tales . . . Tell me, whose books do you read?'

'Oh, Maugham, Priestley, Thurber. And among

the older lot, Bennett and Wells . . .' I hesitated, groping for an important name, and I noticed a shadow, a sad shadow, pass across my companion's face.

'Oh yes, and Kipling,' I said. 'I read a lot of Kipling.'

His face brightened up at once and the eyes behind the thick-lensed spectacles suddenly came to life.

'I'm Kipling,' he said.

I stared at him in astonishment. And then, realizing that he might perhaps be dangerous, I smiled feebly and said, 'Oh yes?'

'You probably don't believe me. I'm dead, of course.'

'So I thought.'

'And you don't believe in ghosts?'

'Not as a rule.'

'But you'd have no objection to talking to one if he came along?'

'I'd have no objection. But how do I know you're Kipling? How do I know you're not an impostor?'

'Listen, then:

When my heavens were turned to blood,
When the dark had filled my day,
Furthest, but most faithful, stood
That lone star I cast away.
I had loved myself, and I
Have not lived and dare not die.

'Once,' he said, gripping me by the arm and looking me straight in the eye. 'Once in life I watched a star but I whistled her to go.'

'Your star hasn't fallen yet,' I said, suddenly moved, suddenly quite certain that I sat beside Kipling. 'One day, when there is a new spirit of adventure abroad, we will discover you again.'

'Why have they heaped scorn on me for so long?'

'You were too militant, I suppose—too much of an Empire man. You were too patriotic for your own good.'

He looked a little hurt. 'I was never very political,' he said. 'I wrote over 600 poems. And you could only call a dozen of them political. I have been abused for harping on the theme of the White Man's burden but my only aim was to show off the Empire to my audience—and I believed the Empire was a fine and noble thing. Is it wrong to believe in something? I never went deeply into political issues, that's true. You must remember, my seven years in India were very youthful years. I was in my twenties, a little immature if you like, and my interest in India was a boy's interest. Action appealed to me more than anything else. You must understand that.'

'No one has described action more vividly, or India so well. I feel at one with Kim wherever he goes along the Grand Trunk Road, in the temples at Banaras, amongst the Saharanpur fruit gardens, on the snow-covered Himalayas. *Kim* has colour and movement and poetry.'

He sighed and a wistful look came into his eyes.

'I'm prejudiced, of course,' I continued. 'I've spent most of my life in India—not *your* India, but an India that does still have much of the colour and atmosphere that you captured. You know, Mr Kipling, you can still sit in a third-class railway carriage and meet the most wonderful assortment of people. In any village you will still find the same courtesy, dignity and courage that the Lama and Kim found on their travels.'

'And the Grand Trunk Road? Is it still a long winding procession of humanity?'

'Well, not exactly,' I said a little ruefully. 'It's just a procession of motor vehicles now. The poor Lama would be run down by a truck if he became too dreamy on the Grand Trunk Road. Times *have* changed. There are no more Mrs Hawksbees in Simla, for instance.'

There was a faraway look in Kipling's eyes. Perhaps he was imagining himself a boy again. Perhaps he could see the hills or the red dust of Rajputana. Perhaps he was having a private conversation with Privates Mulvaney and Ortheris, or perhaps he was out hunting with the Seonce wolf-pack. The sound of London's traffic came to us through the glass doors but we heard only the creaking of bullock-cart wheels and the distant music of a flute.

He was talking to himself, repeating a passage from one of his stories. 'And the last puff of the daywind brought from the unseen villages the scent of damp wood-smoke, hot cakes, dripping undergrowth, and rotting pine-cones. That is the true smell of the Himalayas and if once it creeps into the blood of a man, that man will at the last, forgetting all else, return to the hills to die.'

A mist seemed to have risen between us—or had it come in from the streets?—and when it cleared, Kipling had gone away.

I asked the gatekeeper if he had seen a tall man with a slight stoop, wearing spectacles.

'Nope,' said the gatekeeper. 'Nobody's been by for the last ten minutes.'

'Did someone like that come into the gallery a little while ago?'

'No one that I recall. What did you say the bloke's name was?'

'Kipling,' I said.

'Don't know him.'

'Didn't you ever read *The Jungle Books*?'

'Sounds familiar. Tarzan stuff, wasn't it?'

I left the museum and wandered about the streets for a long time but I couldn't find Kipling anywhere. Was it the boom of London's traffic that I heard or the boom of the Sutlej river racing through the valleys?

Tribute to a Dead Friend

NOW THAT THANH is dead, I suppose it is not too treacherous of me to write about him. It is supposed to be in very bad taste to discuss a person behind his back and to discuss a dead person is most unfair, for he cannot even retaliate. But Thanh had this very weakness of criticizing absent people and it cannot hurt him now if I do a little to expose his colossal ego.

Thanh was a fraud all right but no one knew it. He had beautiful round eyes, a flashing smile and a sweet voice and everyone said he was a charming person. He was certainly charming but I have found that charming people are seldom sincere. I think I was the only person who came anywhere near to being his friend for he had cultivated a special loneliness of his own and it was difficult to intrude on it.

I met him in London in the summer of '54. Though it was only my second year in London I was already longing for the hills and rivers of India. Thanh was Vietnamese. His family was well-to-do and though the Communists had taken their home-town of Hanoi, most of the family was in France, well-established in the restaurant business. Thanh did not suffer from the same financial distress as other students whose homes were in Northern Vietnam. He wasn't studying anything in particular but practised assiduously on the piano, though the only thing he could play fairly well was Chopin's *Funeral March*.

My friend Pravin, a happy-go-lucky, very friendly Gujarati boy, introduced me to Thanh. Pravin, like a good Indian, thought all Asians were superior people, but he didn't know Thanh well enough to know that Thanh didn't like being an Asian.

At first, Thanh was glad to meet me. He said he had for a long time been wanting to make friends with an Englishman, a real Englishman, not one who was a Pole, a Cockney or a Jew; he was most anxious to improve his English and talk like Mr Glendenning of the BBC. Pravin, knowing that I had been born and bred in India, suppressed his laughter with some difficulty. But Thanh was soon disillusioned. My accent was anything but English. It was a pronounced *chi-chi* accent.

'You speak like an Indian!' exclaimed Thanh, horrified. 'Are you an Indian?'

'He's Welsh,' said Pravin with a wink.

Thanh was slightly mollified. Being Welsh was the next best thing to being English. Only he disapproved of the Welsh for speaking with an Indian accent.

Later, when Pravin had gone, and I was sitting in Thanh's room drinking Chinese tea, he confided in me that he disliked Indians.

'Isn't Pravin your friend?' I asked.

'I don't trust him,' he said. 'I have to be friendly with him but I don't trust him at all. I don't trust any Indians.'

'What's wrong with them?'

'They are too inquisitive,' complained Thanh. 'No sooner have you met one of them than he is asking you who your father is, and what your job is, and how much money you have in the bank.'

I laughed and tried to explain that in India inquisitiveness is a sign of a desire for friendship, and that he should feel flattered when asked such personal questions. I protested that I was an Indian myself and he said if that was so he wouldn't trust me either.

But he seemed to like me and often invited me to his rooms. He could make some wonderful Chinese and French dishes. When we had eaten, he would sit down at his second-hand piano and play Chopin. He always complained that I didn't listen properly.

He complained of my untidiness and my

unwarranted self-confidence. It was true that I appeared most confident when I was not very sure of myself. I boasted of an intimate knowledge of London's geography but I was an expert at losing my way and then blaming it on someone else.

'You are a useless person,' said Thanh, while with chopsticks I stuffed my mouth with delicious pork and fried rice. 'You cannot find your way anywhere. You cannot speak English properly. You do not know anyone here. How are you going to be a writer?'

'If I am as bad as all that,' I said, 'why do you remain my friend?'

'I want to study your stupidity,' he said.

That was why he never made any real friends. He loved to work out your faults and examine your imperfections. There was no such thing as a real friend, he said. He had looked everywhere but he could not find the perfect friend.

'What is your idea of a perfect friend?' I asked him. 'Does he have to speak perfect English?'

But sarcasm was only wasted on Thanh—he admitted that perfect English was one of the requisites of a perfect friend!

Sometimes, in moments of deep gloom, he would tell me that he did not have long to live.

'There is a pain in my chest,' he complained. 'There is something ticking there all the time. Can you hear it?'

He would bare his bony chest for me and I would put my ear to the offending spot. But I could never hear any ticking.

'Visit the hospital,' I advised. 'They'll give you an X-ray and a proper check-up.'

'I have had X-rays,' he lied. 'They never show anything.'

Then he would talk of killing himself. This was his theme song: he had no friends, he was a failure as a musician, there was no other career open to him, he hadn't seen his family for five years, and he couldn't go back to Indo-China because of the Communists. He magnified his own troubles and minimized other people's troubles. When I was in hospital with an old acquaintance, amoebic dysentery, Pravin came to see me every day. Thanh, who was not very busy, came only once and never again. He said the hospital ward depressed him.

'You need a holiday,' I told him when I was out of hospital. 'Why don't you join the students' union and work on a farm for a week or two? That should toughen you up.'

To my surprise, the idea appealed to him and he got ready for the trip. Suddenly, he became suffused with goodwill towards all mankind. As evidence of his trust in me, he gave me the key of his room to keep (though he would have been secretly delighted if

I had stolen his piano and chopsticks, giving him the excuse to say 'never trust an Indian or an Anglo-Indian'), and introduced me to a girl called Vu-Phuong, a small, very pretty Annamite girl who was studying at the Polytechnic. Miss Vu, Thanh told me, had to leave her lodgings next week and would I find somewhere else for her to stay? I was an experienced hand at finding bed-sitting rooms, having changed my own abode five times in two years (that sweet, nomadic London life!). As I found Miss Vu very attractive, I told her I would get her a room, one not far from my own, in case she needed any further assistance.

Later, in confidence, Thanh asked me not to be too friendly with Vu-Phuong as she was not to be trusted.

But as soon as he left for the farm, I went round to see Vu in her new lodgings which were one tube-station away from my own. She seemed glad to see me and as she too could make French and Chinese dishes I accepted her invitation to lunch. We had chicken noodles, soya sauce and fried rice. I did the washing-up. Vu said: 'Do you play cards, Rusty?' She had a sweet, gentle voice that brought out all the gallantry in a man. I began to feel protective and hovered about her like a devoted cocker spaniel.

'I'm not much of a card-player,' I said.

'Never mind, I'll tell your fortune with them.'

She made me shuffle the cards. Then scattered them about on the bed in different patterns. I would be very rich, she said. I would travel a lot and I would reach the age of forty. I told her I was comforted to know it.

The month was June and Hampstead Heath was only ten minutes' walk from the house. Boys flew kites from the hill and little painted boats scurried about on the ponds. We sat down on the grass, on the slope of the hill, and I held Vu's hand.

For three days I ate with Vu and we told each other our fortunes as we lay on the grass on Hampstead Heath. On the fourth day she told me that she was going to Berkshire and would be back only after a fortnight. When she returned, I said, 'Vu, I would like to marry you.'

'I will think about it,' she said.

Thanh came back on the sixth day and said, 'You know, Rusty, I have been doing some thinking and Vu is not such a bad girl after all. I will ask her to marry me. That is what I need—a wife!'

'Why didn't you think of it before?' I said. 'When will you ask her?'

'Tonight,' he said. 'I will come to see you afterwards and tell you if I have been successful.'

I shrugged my shoulders resignedly and waited. Thanh left me at six in the evening and I waited for him till ten o'clock, all the time feeling a little sorry for him. More disillusionment for Thanh! Poor Thanh . . .

He came in at ten o'clock, his face beaming. He slapped me on the back and said I was his best friend.

'Did you ask her?' I said.

'Yes. She said she would think about it. That is the same as "yes".'

'It isn't,' I said, unfortunately for both of us. 'She told me the same thing.'

Thanh looked at me as though I had just stabbed him in the back. *Et tu* Rusty was what his expression said.

We took a taxi and sped across to Vu's rooms. The uncertain nature of her replies was too much for both of us. Without a definite answer neither of us would have been able to sleep that night.

Vu was not at home. The landlady met us at the door and told us that Vu had gone to the theatre with an Indian gentleman.

Thanh gave me a long, contemptuous look.

'Never trust an Indian,' he said.

'Never trust a woman,' I replied.

At twelve o'clock I woke Pravin. Whenever I could not sleep, I went to Pravin. He knew the remedy for all ailments. As on previous occasions, he went to the cupboard and produced a bottle of cognac. We got drunk.

Three weeks later Thanh went to Paris to help in his sister's restaurant. I did not hear from Vu-Phuong for some time.

A couple of months later, Pravin brought the news that Thanh was dead. He didn't have any details; all he could tell me was that Thanh died of some unknown disease. I wonder if it had anything to do with the ticking in his chest or with his vague threats of suicide. I doubt if I will ever know. And I will never know how much I hated Thanh, and how much I liked him, or if there was any difference between hating and liking him.

The Girl from Copenhagen

I DON'T KNOW why exactly I fell in love with Vu-Phuong. Maybe it is quite simple at that age to fall in love with someone, and Vu was the sort of girl—pretty, soft-spoken, demure—who could enslave me without any apparent effort.

She was happy to accompany me on walks across Hampstead Heath and over Primrose Hill. It was summer time and the grass smelt sweet and was good to lie upon. We lay close to each other and watched boys flying kites. No one bothered us. She put her hand in mine. I walked her home and she made tea for me.

We went about together. She said she looked upon me as a friend, a brother (fatal word!), and would depend upon me for many things. When she went away for a fortnight, I was desolate. It was only as far as a farm in Berkshire where she had joined some other girl students picking strawberries. On a Sunday I took a train to Newbury and then a small branch line to the village of Kintbury—a pretty little place with an old inn, a couple of small shops and plenty of farmland. I had Vu's address, and after lunching at the inn, I set off for the farm where Vu and her friends were working. It was a lovely summer's day, and my first walk in the English countryside.

It took me back to a favourite story, H.E. Bates's *Alexander*, and some of his Uncle Silas tales. Although I had walked all over London, this was different, and I wished now that I had spent more time in the country and less in the city.

Vu seemed happy to see me but she was equally happy among her friends—those fresh-faced, healthy-looking English schoolgirls—and obviously enjoyed living on the farm and picking strawberries. I don't suppose there could have been a better way of earning enough money for college and hostel fees. I walked back to Kintbury alone and reached Charing Cross station late at night. I spent an hour in one of those little news theatres which interspersed newsreels with cartoon shows; supped off station coffee and sandwiches; and then took the last train to Swiss Cottage.

When she got back to London I asked Vu if she'd marry me. As you know, she didn't say yes and she didn't say no. Nor did she ask me if I had any prospects, because it was obvious I had none. But she did say she would think about it and have to talk to her parents about it and they were in Haiphong, in North Vietnam, and she hadn't heard from them for several months. The war in Vietnam had just started and it was to last a long time.

I had to be patient, it seemed, very patient. Of course, the fact that she had given the same response to Thanh's proposal only made matters even more confusing and perplexing. To top it all, Vu herself wasn't to be found.

A few days after I heard about Thanh's death, Vu resurfaced and introduced me to Ulla, a sixteen-year-old Danish girl who had come over to England for a holiday.

'Please look after Ulla for a few days,' said Vu. 'She doesn't know anyone in London.'

'But I want to look after you,' I protested. Why was she foisting this girl on me? Was it possible that she had conceived of Ulla as a device to get rid of me?

'This is Ulla,' said Vu, thrusting a blonde child into my arms. 'Bye and don't get up to any mischief!'

Vu disappeared, and I was left alone with Ulla at the entrance to the Charing Cross Underground Station. She grinned at me and I smiled back rather nervously. She had blue eyes and a smooth, tanned skin. She was small for a Scandinavian girl, reaching only to my shoulders, and her figure was slim and boyish. She was carrying a small travel-bag. It gave me an excuse to do something.

'We'd better leave your bag somewhere,' I said, taking it from her.

And after depositing it in the left-luggage office, we were back on the pavement, grinning at each other.

'Well, Ulla,' I said, 'how many days do you have in London?'

'Only two. Then I go back to Copenhagen.'

'Good. Well, what would you like to do?'

'Eat. I'm hungry.'

I wasn't hungry but there's nothing like a meal to help two strangers get acquainted. We went to a small and not very expensive Indian restaurant off Fitzroy Square and burnt our tongues on an orange-coloured Hyderabad chicken curry. We had to cool off with a Tamil Koykotay before we could talk.

'What do you do in Copenhagen?' I asked.

'I go to school. I'm joining the University next year.'

'And your parents?'

'They have a bookshop.'

'Then you must have done a lot of reading.'

'Oh, no, I don't read much. I can't sit in one place for long. I like swimming and tennis and going to the theatre.'

'But you have to sit in a theatre.'

'Yes, but that's different.'

'It's not sitting that you mind but sitting and reading.'

'Yes, you are right. But most Danish girls like reading—they read more books than English girls.'

'You are probably right,' I said.

As I was out of a job just then and had time on my hands, we were able to feed the pigeons in Trafalgar Square and while away the afternoon in a coffee-bar before going on to a theatre. Ulla was wearing tight jeans and an abbreviated duffle coat and as she had brought little else with her, she wore this outfit to the theatre. It created quite a stir in the foyer but Ulla was completely unconscious of the stares she received. She enjoyed the play, laughed loudly in all the wrong places, and clapped her hands when no one else did.

The lunch and the theatre had lightened my wallet and dinner consisted of baked beans on toast in a small snack-bar. After picking up Ulla's bag, I offered to take her back to Vu's place.

'Why there?' she said. 'Vu must have gone to bed.'

'Yes, but aren't you staying with her?'

'Oh, no. She did not ask me.'

'Then where are you staying? Where have you kept the rest of your things?'

'Nowhere. This is all I brought with me,' she said, indicating the travel-bag.

'Well, you can't sleep on a park bench,' I said. 'Shall I get you a room in a hotel?'

'I don't think so. I have only the money to return to Copenhagen.' She looked crestfallen for a few moments. Then she brightened and slipped her arm through mine. 'I know, I'll stay with you. Do you mind?'

'No, but my landlady—' I began, then stopped. It would have been a lie. My landlady, a generous, broad-minded soul, would not have minded in the least.

'All right,' I said. 'I don't mind.'

When we reached my room in Swiss Cottage Ulla threw off her coat and opened the window wide. It was a warm summer's night and the scent of honeysuckle came through the open window. She kicked her shoes off and walked about the room barefoot. Her toenails were painted a bright pink.

She slipped into bed and said, 'Aren't you coming?'

I crept in beside her and lay very still while she chattered on about the play and the friends she had made in the country. I switched off the bed-lamp and she fell silent. Then she said, 'Well, I'm sleepy. Goodnight!' And turning over, she immediately fell asleep.

I lay awake beside her for some time, after which sleep overcame me and I woke up only when the sun streamed in through the window. Ulla woke fresh and frolicsome. I busied myself with the breakfast. Ulla ate three eggs and a lot of bacon and drank two cups of coffee. I couldn't help admiring her appetite.

'And what shall we do today?' she asked, her blue eyes shining. They were the bright blue eyes of a Siamese kitten.

'I have to go to the library,' I said.

'Can't you go tomorrow—after I have left?'

'If you like.'

'I like.'

And she gave me a swift, unsettling kiss.

We climbed Primrose Hill and watched boys flying kites. We lay in the sun and chewed blades of grass and then we visited the zoo where Ulla fed the monkeys. She consumed innumerable ices. We lunched at a small Greek restaurant and I forgot to phone Vu and in the evening we walked all the way home through scruffy Camden Town, drank beer, ate a fine, greasy dinner of fish and chips and went to bed early—Ulla had to catch the boat-train the next morning.

'It has been a good day,' she said.

'I'd like to do it again tomorrow.'

'But I must go tomorrow.'

'But you must go.'

She turned her head on the pillow and looked

deep into my eyes, as though she were searching for something. I don't know if she found what she was looking for but she smiled and kissed me softly on the lips.

'Thanks for everything,' she said.

'Goodnight Ulla.'

The next morning the station and the train were crowded and we held hands and grinned at each other.

'Give my love to Vu,' she said.

'I will.'

We made no promises—of writing, or of meeting again. Somehow our relationship seemed complete and whole and I passed the day in a glow of happiness. I felt as if Ulla was still with me and it was only at night, when I put my hand out for hers, and did not find it, that I knew she had gone.

But I kept the window open all through the summer and the scent of the honeysuckle was with me every night.

Vu had also vanished from the scene. After a few months I heard from her. She sent a postcard from Paris saying she was staying with her sister for a time and they would be returning to Vietnam together to see their parents.

I kept that postcard for a long time. The stamp bore a picture of Joan of Arc looking like Michele

Morgan in one of her early films.

The day I received it I took a day off from the office and went to a pub and drank several large brandies. They didn't do me any good, so I switched to Jamaica rum and all that it did was make me think of Vu and, of course, I never saw her again.

Return to Dehra

AFTER THE INSULARITY of Jersey, London had been liberating. Theatres, cinemas, bookshops, museums, libraries helped further my self-education. Not once did I give serious thought to joining a college and picking up a degree. In any case, I did not have the funds, and there was no one to sponsor me. Instead, I had to join the vast legion of the world's workers. But Kensington Gardens, Regent's Park, Hampstead Heath and Primrose Hill gave me the green and open spaces that I needed in order to survive. In many respects London was a green city. My forays into the East End were really in search of literary landmarks.

And yet something was missing from my life. Vu-Phuong had come and gone like the breath of wind after which she had been named. And there was no one to take her place.

The affection, the camaraderie, the easy-going pleasures of my Dehra friendships; the colour and atmosphere of India; the feeling of *belonging*—these things I missed . . .

Even though I had grown up with a love for the English language and its literature, even though my forefathers were British, Britain was not really my place. I did not belong to the bright lights of Piccadilly and Leicester Square; or, for that matter, to the apple orchards of Kent or the strawberry fields of Berkshire. I belonged, very firmly, to peepal trees and mango groves; to sleepy little towns all over India; to hot sunshine, muddy canals, the pungent scent of marigolds; the hills of home; spicy odours, wet earth after summer rain, neem pods bursting; laughing brown faces; and the intimacy of human contact.

Human contact! That was what I missed most. It was not to be found in the office where I worked, or in my landlady's house, or in any of the learned societies which I had joined, or even in the pubs into which I sometimes wandered . . . The freedom to touch someone without being misunderstood. To take someone by the hand as a mark of affection rather than desire. Or even to know desire. And fulfilment. To be among strangers without feeling like an outsider. For in India there are no strangers . . .

I had been away for over four years but the bonds were as strong as ever, the longing to return had never left me.

How I expected to make a living in India when I returned was something of a mystery to me. You did not just walk into the nearest employment exchange to find a job waiting for you. I had no qualifications. All I could do was write and I was still a novice at that. If I set myself up as a freelance writer and bombarded every magazine in the country, I could probably eke out a livelihood. At that time there were only some half-a-dozen English language magazines in India and almost no book publishers (except for a handful of educational presses left over from British days). The possibilities were definitely limited; but this did not deter me. I had confidence in myself (too much, perhaps) and plenty of guts (my motto being, 'Never despair. But if you do, work on in despair'). And, of course, all the optimism of youth.

As Donna Stephen and Antony Dahl kept telling me they would publish my novel one day (I had finally put my foot, or rather, my pen, down and refused to do any more work on it), I wheedled a fifty-pound advance out from them, this being the standard advance against royalties at the time. Out of this princely sum I bought a ticket for Bombay on the *S.S. Batory*, a Polish passenger liner which had seen better days. There was a fee for a story I'd sold to the BBC and some money saved from my Photax salary; and with these amounts I bought a decent-looking suitcase and a few presents to take home.

I did not say goodbye to many people—just my office colleagues who confessed that they would miss my imitations of Sir Harry Lauder; and my landlady, to whom I gave my Eartha Kitt records—and walked up the gangway of the *Batory* on a chilly day early in October.

Soon we were in the warmer waters of the Mediterranean and a few days later in the even warmer Red Sea. It grew gloriously hot. But the *Batory* was a strange ship, said to be jinxed. A few months earlier, most of its Polish crew had sought political asylum in Britain. And now, as we passed through the Suez Canal, a crew member jumped overboard and was never seen again. Hopefully he'd swum ashore.

Then, when we were in the Arabian Sea, we had to get out of our bunks in the middle of the night for the ship's alarm bells were ringing and we thought the *Batory* was sinking. As there had been no lifeboat drill and no one had any idea of how a lifebelt should be worn, there was a certain amount of panic. Cries of 'Abandon ship!' mingled with shouts of 'Man overboard!' and 'Women and children first!'—although there were no signs of women and children being given that privilege. Finally it transpired that a passenger, tipsy on too much Polish vodka, had indeed fallen overboard. A lifeboat was lowered and the ship drifted around for some time; but whether or not the passenger was rescued, we were not told. Nor did I discover his (or her) identity. Whatever tragedy had occurred had been swallowed up in the immensity of the darkness and the sea.

The saga of the *Batory* was far from over.

No sooner had the ship docked at Bombay's Ballard Pier than a fire broke out in the hold. Most of the passengers lost their heavy luggage. Fortunately, my suitcase and typewriter were both with me and these I clung to all the way to the Victoria Terminus and all the way to Dehra Dun. I knew it would be some time before I could afford more clothes or another typewriter.

When the train drew into Dehra I found Devinder waiting to greet me. (Somi and Ranbir were now both in Calcutta.)

Devinder had come on his cycle.

I got up on the crossbar of Devinder's bike and he took me to his place (he was staying in the outhouse of a tea-planter) in style, through the familiar streets of the town that had so shaped my life.

The Odeon was showing an old Bogart film; the small roadside cafés were open; the bougainvillaea were a mass of colour; the mango blossoms smelt sweet; Devinder chattered away; and the girls looked prettier than ever.

And I was twenty-four that year.

The Garlands on His Brow

Fame has but a fleeting hold
on the reins in our fast-paced society;
so many of yesterday's
heroes crumble.

SHORTLY AFTER MY return from London, I was walking down the main road of my old hometown of Dehra, gazing at the shops and passers-by to see what changes, if any, had taken place during my absence. I had been away three years. I had returned with some mediocre qualifications to flaunt in the faces of my envious friends. (I did not tell them of the loneliness of those years in exile; it would not have impressed them.) I was nearing the clock tower when I met a beggar coming from the opposite direction. In one respect, Dehra had not changed. The beggars were as numerous as ever, though I had to admit they looked healthier.

This beggar had a straggling beard, a hunch, a

cavernous chest, and unsteady legs on which a number of purple sores were festering. His shoulders looked as though they had once been powerful, and his hands thrusting a begging-bowl at me, were still strong.

He did not seem sufficiently decrepit to deserve of my charity, and I was turning away when I thought I discerned a gleam of recognition in his eyes. There was something slightly familiar about the man; perhaps he was a beggar who remembered me from earlier years. He was even attempting a smile; showing me a few broken yellow fangs; and to get away from him, I produced a coin, dropped it in his bowl, and hurried away.

I had gone about a hundred yards when, with a rush of memory, I knew the identity of the beggar. He was a hero of my adolescence, Hassan, the most magnificent wrestler in the entire district. My friend Hathi used to train under Hassan's guidance and whenever I went to meet Hathi, Hassan would give me a resounding thump on my shoulders and advice me to get into shape.

I turned back (and away from my memories) and retraced my steps, half hoping I wouldn't be able to catch up with the man and he had indeed got lost in the bazaar crowd. Well, I would doubtless be confronted by him again in a day or two . . . . Leaving the road, I went into the municipal gardens and

stretching myself out on the fresh green February grass, allowed my memory to journey back to the days when I was a teenager, full of health and optimism, when my wonder at the great game of living had yet to give way to disillusionment at its shabbiness.

I would sometimes make my way to the akhara at the corner of the gardens to watch the wrestling pit. My chin cupped in my hands, I would lean against a railing and gaze in awe at the wrestlers' rippling muscles, applauding with the other watchers whenever one of them made a particularly clever move or pinned an opponent down on his back.

Amongst these wrestlers the most impressive and engaging young man was Hassan, the son of a kite-maker. He had a magnificent build, with great wide shoulders and powerful legs, and what he lacked in skill he made up for in sheer animal strength and vigour. The idol of all boys, he was followed about by large numbers of us, and I was a particular favourite of his. He would offer to lift me on to his shoulders and carry me across the akhara to introduce me to his friends and fellow-wrestlers. But I was content to be the friend of another wrestler, and that too someone who was about the same age as I was. And that wrestler was Hathi.

From being Dehra's champion, Hassan soon became the outstanding representative of his art in the

entire district. His technique improved, he began
using his brain in addition to his brawn, and it was
said by everyone that he had the making of a national
champion.

It was during a large fair towards the end of the
rains that destiny took a hand in the shaping of his
life. The Rani of Raunakpur was visiting the fair, and
she stopped to watch the wrestling bouts. When she
saw Hassan stripped and in the ring, she began to take
more than a casual interest in him. It has been said
that the Rani was a woman of a passionate and amoral
nature. She was struck by Hassan's perfect manhood,
and through an official offered him the post of her
personal bodyguard.

The Rani was rich and, in spite of having passed
her fortieth summer, was a warm and attractive
woman. Hassan did not find it difficult to do what
was demanded of him, and on the whole he was
happy in her service. True, he did not wrestle as often
as in the past; but when he did enter a competition,
his reputation and his physique combined to overawe
his opponents, and they did not put up much resistance.
One or two well-known wrestlers were invited to the
district. The Rani paid them liberally, and they
permitted Hassan to throw them out of the ring. Life
in the Rani's house was comfortable and easy, and
Hassan, a simple man, felt himself secure. And it is to

the credit of the Rani (and also of Hassan) that she did not tire of him as quickly as she had of others.

But Ranis, like washerwomen, are mortal; and when a long-standing and neglected disease at last took its toll, robbing her at once of all her beauty, she no longer struggled against it, but allowed it to poison and consume her once magnificent body.

It would be wrong to say that Hassan was heartbroken when she died. He was not a deeply emotional or sensitive person. Though he could attract the sympathy of others, he had difficulty in producing any of his own. His was a kindly but not compassionate nature.

He had served the Rani well, and what he was most aware of now was that he was without a job and without any money. The Raja had his own personal amusements and did not want a wrestler who was beginning to sag a little about the waist.

Times had changed. Hassan's father was dead, and there was no longer a living to be had from making kites; so Hassan returned to doing what he had always done: wrestling. But there was no money to be made at the akhara. It was only in the professional arena that a decent living could be made. And so, when a travelling circus of professionals—a Negro, a Russian, a Cockney-Chinese and a giant Sikh—came to town and offered a hundred rupees and a contract to the challenger who could stay five minutes in the ring with any one of them, Hassan took up the challenge.

He was pitted against the Russian, a bear of a man, who wore a black mask across his eyes; and in two minutes Hassan's Dehra supporters saw their hero slung about the ring, licked in the head and groin, and finally flung unceremoniously through the ropes.

After this humiliation, Hassan did not venture into competitive bouts again. I saw him sometimes at the akhara, where he made a few rupees giving lessons to children. He had a paunch, and folds were beginning to accumulate beneath his chin. I was no longer a regular at the akhara but Hassan always had a smile and a hearty back-slap reserved for me whenever he saw me.

I remember seeing him a few days before I went abroad. He was moving heavily about the akhara; he had lost the lightning swiftness that had once made him invincible. Yes, I told myself,

The garlands wither on your brow;
Then boast no more your mighty deeds . . .

That had been over four years ago. And for Hassan to have been reduced to begging was indeed a sad reflection of both the passing of time and the changing times. Fifty years ago a popular local wrestler would never have been allowed to fall into a state of poverty and neglect. He would have been fed by his old friends and stories would have been told of his legendary prowess. He would not have been forgotten. But those were more leisurely times, when the individual had his place in society, when a man was praised for his past achievement and his failures were tolerated and forgiven. But life had since become fast and cruel and unreflective, and people were too busy counting their gains to bother about the idols of their youth.

It was a few days after my last encounter with Hassan that I found a small crowd gathered at the side of the road, not far from the clock tower. They were staring impassively at something in the drain, at the same time keeping a discreet distance. Joining the group, I saw that the object of their disinterested curiosity was a corpse, its head hidden under a culvert, legs protruding into the open drain. It looked as though the man had crawled into the drain to die, and had done so with his head in the culvert so the world would not witness his last unavailing struggle.

When the municipal workers came in their van, and lifted the body out of the gutter, a cloud of flies and bluebottles rose from the corpse with an angry buzz of protest. The face was muddy, but I recognized the beggar who was Hassan.

In a way, it was a consolation to know that he had

been forgotten, that no one present could recognize the remains of the man who had once looked like a young god. I did not come forward to identify the body. Perhaps I saved Hassan from one final humiliation.

Time Stops at Shamli

THE DEHRA EXPRESS usually drew into Shamli at about five o'clock in the morning, at which time the station would be dimly lit and the jungle across the tracks would just be visible in the faint light of dawn. Shamli was a small station at the foot of the Siwalik hills which lie at the foot of the Himalayas.

The station had only one platform, an office for the station-master, and a waiting-room. The platform boasted a tea stall, a fruit vendor, and a few stray dogs. Not much else was required because the train stopped at Shamli for only five minutes before rushing on into the forests.

Why it stopped at Shamli, I never could tell. Nobody got off the train and nobody got in. There were never any coolies on the platform. But the train would stand there a full five minutes and the guard would blow his whistle and presently Shamli would be left behind and forgotten . . . until I passed that way again. I had passed through the station several times on my trips to and from Delhi, without thinking anything of it

I had gone to Delhi on some work soon after I returned to Dehra from London. On the way back the night train stopped at Shamli.

As chance would have it, the train came into Shamli just as I awoke from a restless sleep. The third-class compartment was crowded beyond capacity and I had been sleeping in an upright position with my back to the lavatory door. Now someone was trying to get into the lavatory. He was obviously hard pressed for time.

'I'm sorry, brother,' I said, moving as much as I could to one side.

He stumbled into the closet without bothering to close the door.

'Where are we now?' I asked the man sitting beside me. He was smoking a strong aromatic beedi.

'Shamli station,' he said, rubbing the palm of a large calloused hand over the frosted glass of the window.

I let the window down and stuck my head out. There was a cool breeze blowing down the platform, a breeze that whispered of autumn in the hills. As usual there was no activity except for the fruit-vendor walking up and down the length of the train with his basket of mangoes balanced on his head. At the tea stall, a kettle was steaming, but there was no one to mind it. I rested my forehead on the window-ledge and let the breeze play on my temples. I had been feeling sick and giddy but there was a wild sweetness in the wind that I found soothing.

'Yes,' I said to myself, 'I wonder what happens in Shamli behind the station walls.'

My fellow passenger offered me a beedi. He was a farmer, I think, on his way to Dehra. He had a long, untidy, sad moustache.

We had been more than five minutes at the station. I looked up and down the platform, but nobody was getting on or off the train. Presently the guard came walking past our compartment.

'What's the delay?' I asked him.

'Some obstruction further down the line,' he said.

'Will we be here long?'

'I don't know what the trouble is. About half an hour at the least.'

My neighbour shrugged and throwing the remains of his beedi out of the window, closed his eyes and immediately fell asleep. I moved restlessly in my seat; the man came out of the lavatory, not so urgently now, and with obvious peace of mind. I closed the door for him.

I stood up and stretched and this stretching of my limbs seemed to set in motion a stretching of the mind and I found myself thinking: 'I am in no hurry to get back to Dehra and I have always wanted to see Shamli behind the station walls. If I get down now, I can spend the day here. It will be better than sitting in this train for another hour. Then in the evening I can catch the next train home.'

In those days I never had the patience to wait for second thoughts and so I began pulling my small suitcase out from under the seat.

The farmer woke up and asked, 'What are you doing, brother?'

'I'm getting out,' I said.

He went to sleep again.

It would have taken at least fifteen minutes to reach the door as people and their belongings cluttered up the passage. So I let my suitcase down from the window and followed it onto the platform.

There was no one to collect my ticket at the barrier because there was obviously no point in keeping a man there to collect tickets from passengers who never came. And anyway, I had a through-ticket to Dehra which I would need in the evening.

I went out of the station and came to Shamli.

Outside the station there was a neem tree and under it stood a tonga. The pony was nibbling at the grass at the foot of the tree. The youth in the front seat was the only human in sight. There were no signs of inhabitants or habitation. I approached the tonga and the youth stared at me as though he couldn't believe his eyes.

'Where is Shamli?' I asked.

'Why, friend, this is Shamli,' he said.

I looked around again but couldn't see any sign of life. A dusty road led past the station and disappeared into the forest.

'Does anyone live here?' I asked.

'I live here,' he said with an engaging smile. He looked an amiable, happy-go-lucky fellow. He wore a cotton tunic and dirty white pyjamas.

'Where?' I asked.

'In my tonga, of course,' he said. 'I have had this pony five years now. I carry supplies to the hotel. But today the manager has not come to collect them. You are going to the hotel? I will take you.'

'Oh, so there's a hotel?'

'Well, friend, it is called that. And there are a few houses too and some shops, but they are all about a mile from the station. If they were not a mile from here, I would be out of business.'

I felt relieved but I still had the feeling of having walked into a town consisting of one station, one pony and one man.

'You can take me,' I said. 'I'm staying till this evening.

He heaved my suitcase into the seat beside him and I climbed in at the back. He flicked the reins and slapped his pony on the buttocks and, with a roll and a lurch, the buggy moved off down the dusty forest road.

'What brings you here?' asked the youth.

'Nothing,' I said. 'The train was delayed. I was feeling bored. And so I got off.'

He did not believe that but he didn't question me further. The sun was reaching up over the forest but the road lay in the shadow of tall trees—eucalyptus, mango and neem.

'Not many people stay in the hotel,' he said. 'So it is cheap. You will get a room for five rupees.'

'Who is the manager?'

'Mr Satish Dayal. It is his father's property. Satish Dayal could not pass his exams or get a job so his father sent him here to look after the hotel.'

The jungle thinned out and we passed a temple, a mosque, a few small shops. There was a strong smell of burnt sugar in the air and in the distance I saw a factory chimney. That, then, was the reason for Shamli's existence. We passed a bullock-cart laden with sugarcane. The road went through fields of cane and maize, and then, just as we were about to re-enter the jungle, the youth pulled his horse to a side road and the hotel came in sight.

It was a small white bungalow with a garden in the front, banana trees at the sides and an orchard of guava trees at the back. We came jingling up to the front veranda. Nobody appeared, nor was there any sign of life on the premises.

'They are all asleep,' said the youth.

I said, 'I'll sit in the veranda and wait.' I got down from the tonga and the youth dropped my case on the veranda steps. Then he stood in front of me, smiling amiably, waiting to be paid.

'Well, how much?' I asked.

'As a friend, only one rupee.'

'That's too much,' I complained. 'This is not Delhi.'

'This is Shamli,' he said. 'I am the only tonga in Shamli. You may not pay me anything, if that is your wish. But then, I will not take you back to the station this evening. You will have to walk.'

I gave him the rupee. He had both charm and cunning, an effective combination.

'Come in the evening at about six,' I said.

'I will come,' he said with an infectious smile. 'Don't worry.' I waited till the tonga had gone round the bend in the road before walking up the veranda steps.

The doors of the house were closed and there were no bells to ring. I didn't have a watch but I judged the time to be a little past six o'clock. The hotel didn't look very impressive. The whitewash was coming off the walls and the cane chairs on the veranda were old and crooked. A stag's head was mounted over the front door but one of its glass eyes had fallen out. I had often heard hunters speak of how beautiful an animal looked before it died, but how could anyone with true love of the beautiful care for the stuffed head of an animal, grotesquely mounted, with no resemblance to its living aspect?

I felt too restless to take any of the chairs. I began pacing up and down the veranda, wondering if I should start banging on the doors. Perhaps the hotel was deserted. Perhaps the tonga-driver had played a trick on me. I began to regret my impulsiveness in leaving the train. When I saw the manager I would have to invent a reason for coming to his hotel. I was good at inventing reasons. I would tell him that a friend of mine had stayed here some years ago and that I was trying to trace him. I decided that my friend would have to be a little eccentric (having chosen Shamli to live in), that he had become a recluse, shutting himself off from the world. His parents—no, his sister—for his parents would be dead— had asked me to find him if I could and, as he had last been heard of in Shamli, I had taken the opportunity to enquire after him. His name would be Major Roberts, retired.

I heard a tap running at the side of the building and walking around found a young man bathing at the tap. He was strong and well-built and slapped himself on the body with great enthusiasm. He had not seen me approaching so I waited until he had finished bathing and had begun to dry himself.

'Hallo,' I said.

He turned at the sound of my voice and looked at me for a few moments with a puzzled expression. He had a round cheerful face and crisp black hair. He smiled slowly. But it was a more genuine smile than the tonga-driver's. So far I had met two people in Shamli and they were both smilers. That should have cheered me, but it didn't. 'You have come to stay?' he asked in a slow easygoing voice.

'Just for the day,' I said. 'You work here?'

'Yes, my name is Daya Ram. The manager is asleep just now but I will find a room for you.'

He pulled on his vest and pyjamas and accompanied me back to the veranda. Here he picked up my suitcase and, unlocking a side door, led me into the house. We went down a passageway. Then Daya Ram stopped at the door on the right, pushed it open and took me into a small, sunny room that had a window looking out onto the orchard. There was a bed, a desk, a couple of cane chairs, and a frayed and faded red carpet.

'Is it all right?' said Daya Ram.

'Perfectly all right.'

'They have breakfast at eight o'clock. But if you are hungry, I will make something for you now.'

'No, it's all right. Are you the cook too?'

'I do everything here.'

'Do you like it?'

'No,' he said. And then added, in a sudden burst of confidence, 'There are no women for a man like me.'

'Why don't you leave, then?'

'I will,' he said with a doubtful look on his face. 'I will leave . . .'

After he had gone I shut the door and went into the bathroom to bathe. The cold water refreshed me and made me feel one with the world. After I had dried myself, I sat on the bed, in front of the open window. A cool breeze, smelling of rain, came through the window and played over my body. I thought I saw a movement among the trees.

And getting closer to the window, I saw a girl on a swing. She was a small girl, all by herself, and she was swinging to and fro and singing, and her song carried faintly on the breeze.

I dressed quickly and left my room. The girl's dress was billowing in the breeze, her pigtails flying about. When she saw me approaching, she stopped swinging and stared at me. I stopped a little distance away.

'Who are you?' she asked.

'A ghost,' I replied.

'You look like one,' she said.

I decided to take this as a compliment, as I was determined to make friends. I did not smile at her because some children dislike adults who smile at them all the time.

'What's your name?' I asked.

'Kiran,' she said. 'I'm ten.'

'You are getting old.'

'Well, we all have to grow old one day. Aren't you coming any closer?'

'May I?' I asked.

'You may. You can push the swing.'

One pigtail lay across the girl's chest, the other behind her shoulder. She had a serious face and obviously felt she had responsibilities. She seemed to be in a hurry to grow up, and I suppose she had no time for anyone who treated her as a child. I pushed the swing until it went higher and higher and then I stopped pushing so that she came lower each time and we could talk.

'Tell me about the people who live here,' I said.

'There is Heera,' she said. 'He's the gardener. He's nearly a hundred. You can see him behind the hedges in the garden. You can't see him unless you look hard.

He tells me stories, a new story every day. He's much better than the people in the hotel and so is Daya Ram.'

'Yes, I met Daya Ram.'

'He's my bodyguard. He brings me nice things from the kitchen when no one is looking.'

'You don't stay here?'

'No, I live in another house. You can't see it from here. My father is the manager of the factory.'

'Aren't there any other children to play with?' I asked.

'I don't know any,' she said.

'And the people staying here?'

'Oh, *they*.' Apparently Kiran didn't think much of the hotel guests. 'Miss Deeds is funny when she's drunk. And Mr Lin is the *strangest*.'

'And what about the manager, Mr Dayal?'

'He's mean. And he gets frightened of the slightest things. But Mrs Dayal is nice. She lets me take flowers home. But she doesn't talk much.'

I was fascinated by Kiran's ruthless summing up of the guests. I brought the swing to a standstill and asked, 'And what do you think of me?'

'I don't know as yet,' said Kiran quite seriously. 'I'll think about you.'

As I came back to the hotel, I heard the sound of a piano in one of the front rooms. I didn't know enough about music to be able to recognize the piece but it had sweetness and melody though it was played with some hesitancy. As I came nearer, the sweetness deserted the music, probably because the piano was out of tune.

The person at the piano had distinctive Mongolian features and so I presumed he was Mr Lin. He hadn't seen me enter the room and I stood beside the curtains of the door, watching him play. He had full round lips and high, slanting cheekbones. His eyes were large and round and full of melancholy. His long, slender fingers hardly touched the keys.

I came nearer and then he looked up at me, without any show of surprise or displeasure, and kept on playing.

'What are you playing?' I asked.

'Chopin,' he said.

'Oh, yes. It's nice but the piano is fighting it.'

'I know. This piano belonged to one of Kipling's aunts. It hasn't been tuned since the last century.'

'Do you live here?'

'No, I come from Calcutta,' he answered readily. 'I have some business here with the sugarcane people, actually, though I am not a businessman.' He was playing softly all the time so that our conversation was not lost in the music. 'I don't know anything about business. But I have to do something.'

'Where did you learn to play the piano?'

'In Singapore. A French lady taught me. She had great hopes of my becoming a concert pianist when I grew up. I would have toured Europe and America.'

'Why didn't you?'

'We left during the War and I had to give up my lessons.'

'And why did you go to Calcutta?'

'My father is a Calcutta businessman. What do you do and why do you come here?' he asked. 'If I am not being too inquisitive.'

Before I could answer, a bell rang, loud and continuously, drowning the music and conversation.

'Breakfast,' said Mr Lin.

A thin dark man, wearing glasses, stepped nervously into the room and peered at me in an anxious manner.

'You arrived last night?'

'That's right,' I said. 'I just want to stay the day. I think you are the manager?'

'Yes. Would you like to sign the register?'

I went with him past the bar and into the office. I wrote my name and Dehra address in the register and the duration of my stay. I paused at the column marked 'Profession', thought it would be best to fill it with something and wrote 'Author'.

'You are here on business?' asked Mr Dayai.

'No, not exactly. You see, I'm looking for a friend

of mine who was last heard of in Shamli, about three years ago. I thought I'd make a few enquiries in case he's still here.'

'What was his name? Perhaps he stayed here.'

'Major Roberts,' I said. 'An Anglo-Indian.'

'Well, you can look through the old registers after breakfast.'

He accompanied me into the dining-room. The establishment was really more of a boarding-house than a hotel because Mr Dayal ate with his guests. There was a round mahogany dining table in the centre of the room and Mr Lin was the only one seated at it. Daya Ram hovered about with plates and trays. I took my seat next to Lin and, as I did so, a door opened from the passage and a woman of about thirty-five came in.

She had on a skirt and blouse which accentuated a firm, well-rounded figure, and she walked on high heels, with a rhythmical swaying of the hips. She had an uninteresting face, camouflaged with lipstick, rouge and powder—the powder so thick that it had become embedded in the natural lines of her face—but her figure compelled admiration.

'Miss Deeds,' whispered Lin.

There was a false note to her greeting.

'Hallo, everyone,' she said heartily, straining for effect. 'Why are you all so quiet? Has Mr Lin been playing the *Funeral March* again?' She sat down and continued talking. 'Really, we must have a dance or something to liven things up. You must know some good numbers, Lin, after your experience of Singapore night-clubs. What's for breakfast? Boiled eggs. Daya Ram, can't you make an omelette for a change? I know you're not a professional cook but you don't have to give us the same thing every day, and there's absolutely no reason why you should burn the toast. You'll have to do something about a cook, Mr Dayal.' Then she noticed me sitting opposite her. 'Oh, hallo,' she said, genuinely surprised. She gave me a long appraising look.

'This gentleman,' said Mr Dayal introducing me, 'is an author.'

'That's nice,' said Miss Deeds. 'Are you married?'

'No,' I said. 'Are you?'

'Funny, isn't it,' she said, without taking offence, 'no one in this house seems to be married.'

'I'm married,' said Mr Dayal.

'Oh, yes, of course,' said Miss Deeds. 'And, what brings you to Shamli?' she asked, turning to me.

'I'm looking for a friend called Major Roberts.'

Lin gave an exclamation of surprise. I thought he had seen through my deception.

But another game had begun.

'I knew him,' said Lin. 'A great friend of mine.'

'Yes,' continued Lin. 'I knew him. A good chap, Major Roberts.'

Well, there I was, inventing people to suit my convenience, and people like Mr Lin started inventing relationships with them. I was too intrigued to try and discourage him. I wanted to see how far he would go.

'When did you meet him?' asked Lin, taking the initiative.

'Oh, only about three years back. Just before he disappeared. He was last heard of in Shamli.'

'Yes, I heard he was here,' said Lin. 'But he went away, when he thought his relatives had traced him. He went into the mountains near Tibet.'

'Did he?' I said, unwilling to be instructed further. 'What part of the country? I come from the hills myself. I know the Mana and Niti passes quite well. If you have any idea of exactly where he went, I think I could find him.' I had the advantage in this exchange because I was the one who had originally invented Roberts. Yet I couldn't bring myself to end Lin's deception, probably because I felt sorry for him. A happy man wouldn't take the trouble of inventing friendships with people who didn't exist. He'd be too busy with friends who did.

'You've had a lonely life, Mr Lin?' I asked.

'Lonely?' said Mr Lin, with forced incredulousness. 'I'd never been lonely till I came here a month ago. When I was in Singapore . . .'

'You never get any letters though, do you?' asked Miss Deeds suddenly.

Lin was silent for a moment. Then he said: 'Do you?'

Miss Deeds lifted her head a little, as a horse does when it is annoyed, and I thought her pride had been hurt, but then she laughed unobtrusively and tossed her head.

'I never write letters,' she said. 'My friends gave me up as hopeless years ago. They know it's no use writing to me because they rarely get a reply. They call me the Jungle Princess.'

Mr Dayal tittered and I found it hard to suppress a smile. To cover up my smile I asked, 'You teach here?'

'Yes, I teach at the girls' school,' she said with a frown. 'But don't talk to me about teaching. I have enough of it all day.'

'You don't like teaching?'

She gave me an aggressive look. 'Should I?' she asked.

'Shouldn't you?' I said.

She paused, and then said, 'Who are you, anyway, the Inspector of Schools?'

'No,' said Mr Dayal who wasn't following very well, 'he's a journalist.'

'I've heard they are nosey,' said Miss Deeds.

Once again Lin interrupted to steer the conversation away from a delicate issue.

'Where's Mrs Dayal this morning?' asked Lin.

'She spent the night with our neighbours,' said Mr Dayal. 'She should be here after lunch.'

It was the first time Mrs Dayal had been mentioned. Nobody spoke either well or ill of her. I suspected that she kept her distance from the others, avoiding familiarity. I began to wonder about Mrs Dayal.

Daya Ram came in from the veranda looking worried.

'Heera's dog has disappeared,' he said. 'He thinks a leopard took it.'

Heera, the gardener, was standing respectfully outside on the veranda steps. We all hurried out to him, firing questions which he didn't try to answer.

'Yes. It's a leopard,' said Kiran appearing from behind Heera. 'It's going to come into the hotel,' she added cheerfully.

'Be quiet,' said Satish Dayal crossly.

'There are pug marks under the trees,' said Daya Ram.

Mr Dayal, who seemed to know little about leopards or pug marks, said, 'I will take a look,' and led the way to the orchard, the rest of us trailing behind in an ill-assorted procession.

There were marks on the soft earth in the orchard (they could have been a leopard's) which went in the direction of the riverbed. Mr Dayal paled a little and went hurrying back to the hotel. Heera returned to the front garden, the least excited, the most sorrowful. Everyone else was thinking of a leopard but he was thinking of the dog.

I followed him and watched him weeding the sunflower beds. His face was wrinkled like a walnut but his eyes were clear and bright. His hands were thin and bony but there was a deftness and power in the wrist and fingers and the weeds flew fast from his spade. He had a cracked, parchment-like skin. I could not help thinking of the gloss and glow of Daya Ram's limbs as I had seen them when he was bathing and wondered if Heera's had once been like that and if Daya Ram's would ever be like this, and both possibilities—or were they probabilities—saddened me. Our skin, I thought, is like the leaf of a tree, young and green and shiny. Then it gets darker and heavier, sometimes spotted with disease, sometimes eaten away. Then fading, yellow and red, then falling, crumbling into dust or feeding the flames of fire. I looked at my own skin, still smooth, not coarsened by labour. I thought of Kiran's fresh rose-tinted complexion; Miss

Deeds's skin, hard and dry; Lin's pale taut skin, stretched tightly across his prominent cheeks and forehead; and Mr Dayal's grey skin growing thick hair. And I wondered about Mrs Dayal and the kind of skin she would have.

'Did you have the dog for long?' I asked Heera.

He looked up with surprise for he had been unaware of my presence.

'Six years, sahib,' he said. 'He was not a clever dog but he was very friendly. He followed me home one day when I was coming back from the bazaar. I kept telling him to go away but he wouldn't. It was a long walk and so I began talking to him. I liked talking to him and I have always talked to him and we have understood each other. That first night, when I came home, I shut the gate between us. But he stood on the other side looking at me with trusting eyes. Why did he have to look at me like that?'

'So you kept him?'

'Yes, I could never forget the way he looked at me. I shall feel lonely now because he was my only companion. My wife and son died long ago. It seems I am to stay here forever, until everyone has gone, until there are only ghosts in Shamli. Already the ghosts are here . . .'

I heard a light footfall behind me and turned to find Kiran. The barefoot girl stood beside the gardener and with her toes began to pull at the weeds.

'You are a lazy one,' said the old man. 'If you want to help me sit down and use your hands.'

I looked at the girl's fair round face and in her bright eyes I saw something old and wise. And I looked into the old man's wise eyes, and saw something forever bright and young. The skin cannot change the eyes. The eyes are the true reflection of a man's age and sensibilities. Even a blind man has hidden eyes.

'I hope we find the dog,' said Kiran. 'But I would like a leopard. Nothing ever happens here.'

'Not now,' sighed Heera. 'Not now . . . Why, once there was a band and people danced till morning, but now . . .' He paused, lost in thought and then said: 'I have always been here. I was here before Shamli.'

'Before the station?'

'Before there was a station, or a factory, or a bazaar. It was a village then, and the only way to get here was by bullock cart. Then a bus service was started, then the railway lines were laid and a station built, then they started the sugar factory, and for a few years Shamli was a town. But the jungle was bigger than the town. The rains were heavy and malaria was everywhere. People didn't stay long in Shamli. Gradually, they went back into the hills. Sometimes I too wanted to go back to the hills, but what is the use when you are old and have no one left in the world except a few flowers in a troublesome garden? I had to choose between the flowers and the hills, and I chose the flowers. I am tired now, and old, but I am not tired of flowers.'

I could see that his real world was the garden; there was more variety in his flower-beds than there was in the town of Shamli. Every month, every day, there were new flowers in the garden, but there were always the same people in Shamli.

I left Kiran with the old man, and returned to my room. It must have been about eleven o'clock.

I was facing the window when I heard my door being opened. Turning, I perceived the barrel of a gun moving slowly round the edge of the door. Behind the gun was Satish Dayal, looking hot and sweaty. I didn't know what his intentions were; so, deciding it would be better to act first and reason later, I grabbed a pillow from the bed and flung it in his face. I then threw myself at his legs and brought him crashing down to the ground.

When we got up, I was holding the gun. It was an old Enfield rifle, probably dating back to Afghan wars, the kind that goes off at the least encouragement.

'But—but—why?' stammered the dishevelled and alarmed Mr Dayal.

'I don't know,' I said menacingly. 'Why did you come in here pointing this at me?'

'I wasn't pointing it at you. It's for the leopard.'

'Oh, so you came into my room looking for a leopard? You have, I presume, been stalking one about the hotel?' (By now I was convinced that Mr Dayal had taken leave of his senses and was hunting imaginary leopards.)

'No, no,' cried the distraught man, becoming more confused. 'I was looking for you. I wanted to ask you if you could use a gun. I was thinking we should go looking for the leopard that took Heera's dog. Neither Mr Lin nor I can shoot.'

'Your gun is not up-to-date,' I said. 'It's not at all suitable for hunting leopards. A stout stick would be more effective. Why don't we arm ourselves with lathis and make a general assault?'

I said this banteringly, but Mr Dayal took the idea quite seriously. 'Yes, yes,' he said with alacrity, 'Daya Ram has got one or two lathis in the godown. The three of us could make an expedition. I have asked Mr Lin but he says he doesn't want to have anything to do with leopards.'

'What about our Jungle Princess?' I said. 'Miss Deeds should be pretty good with a lathi.'

'Yes, yes,' said Mr Dayal humourlessly, 'but we'd better not ask her.'

Collecting Daya Ram and two lathis, we set off for the orchard and began following the pug marks through the trees. It took us ten minutes to reach the riverbed, a dry hot rocky place; then we went into the jungle, Mr Dayal keeping well to the rear. The atmosphere was heavy and humid, and there was not a breath of air amongst the trees. When a parrot squawked suddenly, shattering the silence, Mr Dayal let out a startled exclamation.

'What was that?' he asked nervously.

'A bird,' I explained.

'I think we should go back now,' he said. 'I don't think the leopard's here.'

'You never know with leopards,' I said, 'they could be anywhere.'

Mr Dayal stepped away from the bushes. 'I'll have to go,' he said. 'I have a lot of work. You keep a lathi with you, and I'll send Daya Ram back later.'

'That's very thoughtful of you,' I said.

Daya Ram scratched his head and reluctantly followed his employer back through the trees. I moved on slowly, down the little used path, wondering if I should also return. I saw two monkeys playing on the branch of a tree, and decided that there could be no danger in the immediate vicinity.

Presently I came to a clearing where there was a pool of fresh clear water. It was fed by a small stream that came suddenly, like a snake, out of the long grass. The water looked cool and inviting. Laying down the lathi and taking off my clothes, I ran down the bank until I was waist-deep in the middle of the pool. I splashed about for some time before emerging, then I lay on the soft grass and allowed the sun to dry my body. I closed my eyes and gave myself up to beautiful thoughts. I had forgotten all about leopards.

I must have slept for about half-an-hour because when I awoke, I found that Daya Ram had come back and was vigorously threshing about in the narrow confines of the pool. I sat up and asked him the time.

'Twelve o'clock,' he shouted, coming out of the water, his dripping body all gold and silver in sunlight. 'They will be waiting for lunch.'

'Let them wait,' I said.

It was a relief to talk to Daya Ram, after the uneasy conversations in the lounge and dining-room.

'Dayal sahib will be angry with me.'

'I'll tell him we found the trail of the leopard, and that we went so far into the jungle that we lost our way. As Miss Deeds is so critical of the food, let her cook the meal.'

'Oh, she only talks like that,' said Daya Ram. 'Inside she is very soft. She is too soft in some ways.'

'She should be married.'

'Well, she would like to be. Only there is no one to marry her. When she came here she was engaged to be married to an English army captain. I think she loved him, but she is the sort of person who cannot help loving many men all at once, and the captain could not understand that—it is just the way she is made, I suppose. She is always ready to fall in love.'

'You seem to know,' I said.

'Oh, yes.'

We dressed and walked back to the hotel. In a few hours, I thought, the tonga will come for me and I will be back at the station. The mysterious charm of Shamli will be no more, but whenever I pass this way I will wonder about these people, about Miss Deeds and Lin and Mrs Dayal.

Mrs Dayal . . . She was the one person I had yet to meet. It was with some excitement and curiosity that I looked forward to meeting her; she was about the only mystery left in Shamli, now, and perhaps she would be no mystery when I met her. And yet . . . I felt that perhaps she would justify the impulse that made me get down from the train.

I could have asked Daya Ram about Mrs Dayal, and so satisfied my curiosity; but I wanted to discover her for myself. Half the day was left to me, and I didn't want my game to finish too early.

I walked towards the veranda, and the sound of the piano came through the open door.

'I wish Mr Lin would play something cheerful,' said Miss Deeds. 'He's obsessed with the *Funeral March*. Do you dance?'

'Oh, no,' I said.

She looked disappointed. But when Lin left the piano, she went into the lounge and sat down on the stool. I stood at the door watching her, wondering what she would do. Lin left the room somewhat resentfully.

She began to play an old song which I remembered having heard in a film or on a gramophone record. She sang while she played, in a slightly harsh but pleasant voice:

Rolling round the world
Looking for the sunshine
I know I'm going to find some day . . . .

Then she played *Am I Blue?* and *Darling, Je Vous Aime Beaucoup.* She sat there singing in a deep husky voice, her eyes a little misty, her hard face suddenly kind and sloppy. When the dinner gong rang, she broke off playing and shook off her sentimental mood, and laughed derisively at herself.

I don't remember that lunch. I hadn't slept much since the previous night and I was beginning to feel the strain of my journey. The swim had refreshed me, but it had also made me drowsy. I ate quite well, though, of rice and kofta curry, and then, feeling sleepy, made for the garden to find a shady tree.

There were some books on the shelf in the lounge,

and I ran my eye over them in search of one that might condition sleep. But they were too dull to do even that. So I went into the garden, and there was Kiran on the swing, and I went to her tree and sat down on the grass.

'Did you find the leopard?' she asked.

'No,' I said, with a yawn.

'Tell me a story.'

'You tell me one,' I said.

'All right. Once there was a lazy man with long legs, who was always yawning and wanting to fall asleep . . .'

I watched the swaying motions of the swing and the movements of the girl's bare legs, and a tiny insect kept buzzing about in front of my nose . . .

'. . . And fall asleep, and the reason for this was that he liked to dream . . .'

I blew the insect away, and the swing became hazy and distant, and Kiran was a blurred figure in the trees . . .

'. . . Liked to dream, and what do you think he dreamt about . . .'

Dreamt about, dreamt about . . .

When I awoke there was that cool rain-scented breeze blowing across the garden. I remember lying on the grass with my eyes closed, listening to the swishing of the swing. Either I had not slept long, or Kiran had been a long time on the swing; it was moving slowly now, in a more leisurely fashion, without much sound. I opened my eyes and saw that my arm was stained with the juice of the grass beneath me. Looking up, I expected to see Kiran's legs waving above me. But instead I saw dark slim feet and above them the folds of a sari. I straightened up against the trunk of the tree to look closer at Kiran, but Kiran wasn't there. It was someone else in the swing, a young woman in a pink sari, with a red rose in her hair.

She had stopped the swing with her foot on the ground, and she was smiling at me.

It wasn't a smile you could see, it was a tender fleeting movement that came suddenly and was gone at the same time, and its going was sad. I thought of the others' smiles, just as I had thought of their skins: the tonga-driver's friendly, deceptive smile; Daya Ram's wide sincere smile; Miss Deeds's cynical, derisive smile. And looking at Koki, I knew a smile could never change. She had always smiled that way.

Yes, that was who it was—Koki, the girl I had met one summer in Dehra long, long back. She was a grown-up woman now but I had no difficulty recognizing her.

'You haven't changed,' she said.

I was standing up now, though still leaning against

the tree for support. Though I had never thought much about the sound of her voice, it seemed as familiar as the sounds of yesterday.

'You haven't changed either,' I said. 'But where did you come from?' I wasn't sure yet if I was awake or dreaming.

She laughed as she had always laughed at me.

'I came from behind the tree. The little girl has gone.'

'Yes, I'm dreaming,' I said helplessly.

'But what brings you here?'

'I don't know. At least I didn't know when I came. But it must have been you. The train stopped at Shamli and I don't know why, but I decided I would spend the day here, behind the station walls. You must be married now, Koki.'

'Yes, I am married to Mr Dayal, the manager of the hotel. And what has been happening to you?'

'I am a writer now, and I'm poor, and I still live in Dehra.'

'Is Dehra still the same?' she asked.

'More or less,' I replied. 'Tell me, how have you been?'

'Oh, my friend,' she said, getting up suddenly and coming to me, 'I have been here two years, and I am already feeling old. But now you are here! It was a bit of magic. I came through the trees after Kiran had gone, and there you were, fast asleep under the tree. I didn't wake you then, because I wanted to see you wake up.'

She was near me and I could look at her more closely. Her cheeks did not have the same freshness—they were a little pale—and she was thinner now, but her eyes were the same, smiling the same way. Her fingers, when she took my hand, were the same warm delicate fingers.

'Talk to me,' she said. 'Tell me about yourself.'

'You tell me,' I said.

'I am here,' she said. 'That is all there is to say about myself.'

'Then let us sit down and I'll talk.'

'Not here,' she took my hand and led me through the trees. 'Come with me.'

I heard the jingle of a tonga-bell and a faint shout. I stopped and laughed.

'My tonga,' I said. 'It has come to take me back to the station.'

'But you are not going,' said Koki, immediately downcast.

'I will tell him to come in the morning,' I said. 'I will spend the night in your Shamli.'

I walked to the front of the hotel where the tonga was waiting. I was glad no one else was in sight. The youth was smiling at me in his most appealing manner.

'I'm not going today,' I said. 'Will you come tomorrow morning?'

'I can come whenever you like, friend. But you will have to pay for every trip, because it is a long way from the station even if my tonga is empty. Usual fare, friend, one rupee.'

I didn't try to argue but resignedly gave him the rupee. He cracked his whip and pulled on the reins, and the carriage moved off.

'If you don't leave tomorrow,' the youth called out after me, 'you'll never leave Shamli!'

I walked back through the trees, but I couldn't find Koki.

'Koki, where are you?' I called, but I might have been speaking to the trees, for I had no reply. There was a small path going through the orchard, and on the path I saw a rose petal. I walked a little further and saw another petal. They were from Koki's red rose. I walked on down the path until I had skirted the orchard, and then the path went along the fringe of the jungle, past a clump of bamboos, and here the grass was a lush green as though it had been constantly watered. I was still finding rose petals. I heard the chatter of seven-sisters, and the call of a hoopoe. The path bent to meet a stream, there was a willow coming down to the water's edge, and Koki was sitting there.

'Why didn't you wait?' I said.

'I wanted to see if you were as good at finding your way as you used to be.'

'Well, I am,' I said, sitting down beside her on the grassy bank of the stream. 'Even if I'm a little out of practice.'

'Yes, I remember the time you climbed up an apple tree to pick some fruit for me. You got up all right but then you couldn't come down again. I had to climb up myself and help you.'

'I don't remember that,' I said.

'Of course you do.'

'It must have been some other friend of yours.'

'I never climbed trees with anyone else.'

'Well, I don't remember.'

I looked at the little stream that ran past us. The water was no more than ankle-deep, cold and clear and sparkling, like the mountain-stream near my home. I took off my shoes, rolled up my trousers, and put my feet in the water. Koki's feet joined mine.

At first I had wanted to ask about her marriage, whether she was happy or not, what she thought of her husband; but now I couldn't ask her these things. They seemed far away and of little importance. I could think of nothing she had in common with Mr Dayal. I felt that her charm and attractiveness and warmth could not have been appreciated, or even noticed, by that curiously distracted man. He was much older than her, of course. He was obviously not her choice but her parents', and so far they were childless. Had there been children, I don't think Koki would have minded Mr Dayal as her husband. Children would have made up for the absence of passion—or was there passion in Satish Dayal? . . . I remembered having heard from someone in Dehra that Koki had been married to a man she didn't like. I remembered having shrugged off the news, because it meant she would never come my way again, and I have never yearned after something that has been irredeemably lost. But she *had* come my way again. And was she still lost? That was what I wanted to know . . .

'What do you do with yourself all day?' I asked.

'Oh, I visit the school and help with the classes. It is the only interest I have in this place. The hotel is terrible. I try to keep away from it as much as I can.'

'And what about the guests?'

'Oh, don't let us talk about them. Let us talk about ourselves. Do you *have* to go tomorrow?'

'Yes, I suppose so. Will you always be in this place?'

'I suppose so.'

That made me silent. I took her hand and my feet churned up the mud at the bottom of the stream. As the mud subsided, I saw Koki's face reflected in the water. Suddenly, I wanted to care for her and protect her. I wanted to take her away from that place, from sorrowful Shamli. Of course, I had forgotten all about my poor finances, Koki's family, and the shoes I wore, which were my last pair. The uplift I was experiencing in this meeting with Koki, who had been one of the best friends I had made in all my childhood years, made me reckless and impulsive.

I lifted her hand to my lips and kissed her on the soft of her palm.

She turned her face to me so that we looked deep into each other's eyes, and I kissed her again. And we put our arms around each other and lay together on the grass with the water running over our feet. We said nothing at all, simply lay there for what seemed like several years, or until the first drop of rain.

It was a big wet drop, and it splashed on Koki's cheek just next to mine, and ran down to her lips. The next big drop splattered on the tip of my nose, and Koki laughed and sat up. Little ringlets were forming on the stream where the raindrops hit the water, and above us there was a pattering on the banana leaves.

'We must go,' said Koki.

We started homewards, but had not gone far before it was raining steadily, and Koki's hair came loose and streamed down her body. The rain fell harder, and we had to hop over pools and avoid the soft mud. I pulled her beneath a big tree and held her close, trying to shield her from the rain. I thought she was crying, but I wasn't sure, because it might have been the raindrops on her cheeks.

'Come away with me,' I said impulsively. 'Leave this place. Come away with me tomorrow morning. We will go somewhere far away and be together always.'

She smiled at me and said, 'You are still a dreamer, aren't you?'

'Why can't you come?' I said petulantly.

'I am married. It is as simple as that.'

I didn't know what to say. I felt angry and rebellious, and there was no one and nothing to rebel against.

'I must go back now,' said Koki.

She ran out from under the tree, springing across the grass, and the wet mud flew up and flecked her legs. I watched her through the thin curtain of rain until she reached the veranda. She turned to wave to me, and then skipped into the hotel.

The rain had lessened, but I didn't know what to do with myself. The hotel was uninviting, and it was too late to leave Shamli. If the grass hadn't been wet I would have preferred to sleep under a tree rather than return to the hotel to sit at that alarming dining table.

I came out from under the trees and crossed the garden. But instead of making for the veranda I went round to the back of the hotel. Smoke issuing from the barred window of a back room told me I had probably found the kitchen. Daya Ram was inside, squatting in front of a stove, stirring a pot of stew. The stew smelt appetizing. Daya Ram looked up and smiled at me.

'I thought you had gone,' he said.

'I'll go in the morning,' I said, pulling myself up on an empty table. Then I had one of my sudden ideas and said, 'Why don't you come with me? I can find you a good job in Dehra. How much do you get paid here?'

'Fifty rupees a month. But I haven't been paid for three months.'

'Could you get your pay before tomorrow morning?'

'No, I won't get anything until one of the guests pays a bill. Miss Deeds owes about fifty rupees on whisky alone. She will pay up, she says, when the school pays her salary. And the school can't pay her until they collect the children's fees. That is how bankrupt everyone is in Shamli.'

'I see,' I said, though I didn't see. 'But Mr Dayal can't hold back your pay just because his guests haven't paid their bills.'

'He can if he hasn't got any money.'

'I see,' I said. 'Anyway, I will give you my address. You can come when you are free.'

'I will take it from the register,' he said.

I edged over to the stove and leaning over, sniffed at the stew. 'I'll eat mine now,' I said. And without giving Daya Ram a chance to object, I lifted a plate off the shelf, took hold of the stirring-spoon and helped myself from the pot.

'There's rice too,' said Daya Ram.

I filled another plate with rice and then got busy with my fingers. After ten minutes I had finished. I sat back comfortably, in a ruminative mood. With my stomach full I could take a more tolerant view of life and people. I could understand Mr Dayal's apprehensions, Lin's delicate lying and Miss Deeds's aggressiveness. Daya Ram went out to sound the dinner-gong, and I trailed back to my room.

From the window of my room I saw Kiran running across the lawn and I called to her, but she didn't hear me. She ran down the path and out of the gate, her pigtails beating against the wind.

The clouds were breaking and coming together again, twisting and spiralling their way across a violet sky. The sun was going down behind the Siwaliks. The sky there was bloodshot. The tall slim trunks of the eucalyptus tree were tinged with an orange glow; the rain had stopped, and the wind was a soft, sullen puff, drifting sadly through the trees. There was a steady drip of water from the eaves of the roof onto the window-sill. Then the sun went down behind the old, old hills, and I remembered the hills, far beyond these, that I had trekked to in my teens.

The room was dark but I did not turn on the light. I stood near the window, listening to the garden. There was a frog warbling somewhere and there was a sudden flap of wings overhead. Tomorrow morning I would go, and perhaps I would come back to Shamli one day, and perhaps not. I could always come here looking for Major Roberts, and who knows, one day I might find him. What should he be like, this lost man? A romantic, a man with a dream, a man with brown skin and blue eyes, living in a hut on a snowy mountain-top, chopping wood and catching fish and swimming in cold mountain streams; a rough, free man with a kind heart and a shaggy beard, a man who owed allegiance to no one, who gave a damn for money and politics, and cities and civilizations, who was his own master, who lived at one with nature, knowing no fear. But that was not Major Roberts— that was the man *I* wanted to be. He was not a Frenchman or an Englishman, he was me, a dream of myself. If only I could find Major Roberts.

When Daya Ram knocked on the door and told me the others had finished dinner, I left my room and made for the lounge. It was quite lively in the lounge.

Satish Dayal was at the bar, Lin at the piano, and Miss Deeds in the centre of the room, executing a tango on her own. It was obvious she had been drinking heavily.

'All on credit,' complained Mr Dayal to me. 'I don't know when I'll be paid, but I don't dare refuse her anything for fear she might start breaking up the hotel.'

'She could do that, too,' I said. 'It would come down without much encouragement.'

Lin began to play a waltz (I think it was a waltz), and then I found Miss Deeds in front of me, saying, 'Wouldn't you like to dance, old boy?'

'Thank you,' I said, somewhat alarmed. 'I hardly know how to.'

'Oh, come on, be a sport,' she said, pulling me away from the bar. I was glad Koki wasn't present. She wouldn't have minded, but she'd have laughed as she always laughed when I made a fool of myself.

We went around the floor in what I suppose was waltz-time, though all I did was mark time to Miss Deeds's motions. We were not very steady—this because I was trying to keep her at arm's length, while she was determined to have me crushed to her bosom. At length Lin finished the waltz. Giving him a grateful look, I pulled myself free. Miss Deeds went over to the piano, leaned right across it and said, 'Play something lively, dear Mr Lin, play some hot stuff.'

To my surprise Mr Lin without so much as an

expression of distaste or amusement, began to execute what I suppose was the frug or the jitterbug. I was glad she hadn't asked me to dance that one with her.

It all appeared very incongruous to me: Miss Deeds letting herself go in crazy abandonment, Lin playing the piano with great seriousness, and Mr Dayal watching from the bar with an anxious frown. I wondered what Koki would have thought of them now.

Eventually Miss Deeds collapsed on the couch breathing heavily. 'Give me a drink,' she cried.

With the noblest of intentions I took her a glass of water. Miss Deeds took a sip and made a face. 'What's this stuff?' she asked. 'It is different.'

'Water,' I said.

'No,' she said, 'now don't joke, tell me what it is.'

'It's water, I assure you,' I said.

When she saw that I was serious, her face coloured up and I thought she would throw the water at me. But she was too tired to do this and contented herself with throwing the glass over her shoulder. Mr Dayal made a dive for the flying glass, but he wasn't in time to rescue it and it hit the wall and fell to pieces on the floor.

Mr Dayal wrung his hands. 'You'd better take her to her room,' he said, as though I were personally responsible for her behaviour just because I'd danced with her.

'I can't carry her alone,' I said, making an unsuccessful attempt at helping Miss Deeds up from the couch.

Mr Dayal called for Daya Ram, and the big amiable youth came lumbering into the lounge. We took an arm each and helped Miss Deeds, feet dragging, across the room. We got her to her room and onto her bed. When we were about to withdraw she said, 'Don't go, my dear, stay with me a little while.'

Daya Ram had discreetly slipped outside. With my hand on the door-knob I said, 'Which of us?'

'Oh, are there two of you?' said Miss Deeds, without a trace of disappointment.

'Yes, Daya Ram helped me carry you here.'

'Oh, and who are you?'

'I'm the writer. You danced with me, remember?'

'Of course. You dance divinely, Mr Writer. Do stay with me. Daya Ram can stay too if he likes.'

I hesitated, my hand on the door-knob. She hadn't opened her eyes all the time I'd been in the room, her arms hung loose, and one bare leg hung over the side of the bed. She was fascinating somehow, and desirable, but I was afraid of her. I went out of the room and quietly closed the door.

As I lay awake in bed I heard the jackal's 'pheau', the cry of fear which it communicates to all the jungle when there is danger about, a leopard or a tiger. It was a weird howl, and between each note there was a kind of low gurgling. I switched off the light and peered through the closed window. I saw the jackal at the edge of the lawn. It sat almost vertically on its haunches, holding its head straight up to the sky, making the neighbourhood vibrate with the eerie violence of its cries. Then suddenly it started up and ran off into the trees.

Before getting back into bed I made sure the window was shut. The bull-frog was singing again, 'ing-ong, ing-ong', in some foreign language. I wondered if Koki was awake too, thinking about me. It must have been almost eleven o'clock. I thought of Miss Deeds with her leg hanging over the edge of the bed. I tossed restlessly and then sat up. I hadn't slept for two nights but I was not sleepy. I got out of bed without turning on the light and slowly opening my door, crept down the passageway. I stopped at the door of Miss Deeds's room. I stood there listening, but I heard only the ticking of the big clock that might have been in the room or somewhere in the passage. I put my hand on the door-knob, but the door was bolted.

I would definitely leave Shamli the next morning. Another day in the company of these people and I would be behaving like them. Perhaps I was already doing so! I remembered the tonga-driver's words: 'Don't stay too long in Shamli or you will never leave!'

When the rain came, it was not with a preliminary patter or shower, but all at once, sweeping across the forest like a massive wall, and I could hear it in the trees long before it reached the house. Then it came crashing down on the corrugated roof, and the hailstones hit the window panes with a hard metallic sound so that I thought the glass would break. The sound of thunder was like the booming of big guns and the lightning kept playing over the garden. At every flash of lightning I sighted the swing under the tree, rocking and leaping in the air as though some invisible, agitated being was sitting on it. I wondered about Kiran. Was she sleeping through all this, blissfully unconcerned, or was she lying awake in bed, starting at every clash of thunder as I was? Or was she up and about, exulting in the storm? I half expected to see her come running through the trees, through the rain, to stand on the swing with her hair blowing wild in the wind, laughing at the thunder and the angry skies. Perhaps I did see her, perhaps she was there. I wouldn't have been surprised if she were some forest nymph living in the hole of a tree, coming out sometimes to play in the garden.

A crash, nearer and louder than any thunder so

far, made me sit up in bed with a start. Perhaps lightning had struck the house. I turned on the switch but the light didn't come on. A tree must have fallen across the line.

I heard voices in the passage—the voices of several people. I stepped outside to find out what had happened, and started at the appearance of a ghostly apparition right in front of me. It was Mr Dayal standing on the threshold in an oversized pyjama suit, a candle in his hand.

'I came to wake you,' he said. 'This storm . . .'

He had the irritating habit of stating the obvious.

'Yes, the storm,' I said. 'Why is everybody up?'

'The back wall has collapsed and part of the roof has fallen in. We'd better spend the night in the lounge—it is the safest room. This is a very old building,' he added apologetically.

'All right,' I said. 'I am coming.'

The lounge was lit by two candles. One stood over the piano, the other on a small table near the couch. Miss Deeds was on the couch, Lin was at the piano-stool, looking as though he would start playing Stravinsky any moment, and Dayal was fussing about the room. Koki was standing at a window, looking out at the stormy night. I went to the window and touched her but she didn't look around or say anything. The lightning flashed and her dark eyes were lit up for an instant.

'What time will you be leaving?' she asked.

'The tonga will come for me at seven.'

'If I come,' she said, 'if I come to the station, I will be there before the train leaves.'

'How will you get there?' I asked, excitement rushing over me suddenly.

'I will get there,' she said. 'I will get there before you. But if I am not there, then do not wait, do not come back for me. Go on your way.'

She squeezed my fingers, then drew her hand away. I sauntered over to the next window, then back into the centre of the room. A gust of wind blew through a cracked windowpane and put out the candle near the couch.

'Damn the wind,' said Miss Deeds.

The window in my room had burst open during the night and there were leaves and branches strewn about the floor. I sat down on the damp bed and smelt eucalyptus. The earth was red, as though the storm had bled it all night.

After a little while I went into the veranda with my suitcase to wait for the tonga. It was then that I saw Kiran under the trees. Kiran's long black pigtails were tied up in a red ribbon, and she looked fresh and clean like the rain and the red earth. She stood looking seriously at me.

'Did you like the storm?' she asked.

'Some of the time,' I said. 'I'm going soon. Can I do anything for you?'

'Where are you going?'

'I'm going to the end of the world. I'm looking for Major Roberts, have you seen him anywhere?'

'There is no Major Roberts,' she said perceptively. 'Can I come with you to the end of the world?'

'What about your parents?'

'Oh, we won't take them.'

'They might be annoyed if you go off on your own.'

'I can stay on my own. I can go anywhere.'

'Well, one day I'll come back here and I'll take you everywhere and no one will stop us. Now is there anything else I can do for you?'

'I want some flowers, but I can't reach them,' she pointed to a hibiscus tree that grew against the wall. It meant climbing the wall to reach the flowers. Some of the red flowers had fallen during the night and were floating in a pool of water.

'All right,' I said and pulled myself up on the wall. I smiled down into Kiran's serious, upturned face. 'I'll throw them to you and you can catch them.'

I bent a branch, but the wood was young and green and I had to twist it several times before it snapped.

'I hope nobody minds,' I said, as I dropped the flowering branch to Kiran.

'It's nobody's tree,' she said.

'Sure?'

She nodded vigorously. 'Sure, don't worry.'

I was working for her and she felt immensely capable of protecting me. Talking and being with Kiran, I felt a nostalgic longing for childhood—emotions that had been beautiful because they were never completely understood.

'Who is your best friend?' I said.

'Daya Ram,' she replied. 'I told you so before.'

She was certainly faithful to her friends.

'And who is the second best?'

She put her finger in her mouth to consider the question, and her head dropped sideways.

'I'll make you the second best,' she said.

I dropped the flowers over her head. 'That so kind of you. I'm proud to be your second best.'

I heard the tonga bell, and from my perch on the wall saw the carriage coming down the driveway. 'That's for me,' I said. 'I must go now.'

I jumped down the wall. And the sole of my shoe came off at last.

'I knew that would happen,' I said.

'Who cares for shoes,' said Kiran.

'Who cares,' I said.

I walked back to the veranda and Kiran walked beside me, and stood in front of the hotel while I put my suitcase in the tonga.

'You nearly stayed one day too late,' said the tonga-driver. 'Half the hotel has come down and tonight the other half will come down.'

I climbed into the back seat. Kiran stood on the path, gazing intently at me.

'I'll see you again,' I said.

'I'll see you in Iceland or Japan,' she said. 'I'm going everywhere.'

'Maybe,' I said, 'maybe you will.'

We smiled, knowing and understanding each other's importance. In her bright eyes I saw something old and wise. The tonga-driver cracked his whip, the wheels creaked, the carriage rattled down the path. We kept waving to each other. In Kiran's hand was a spring of hibiscus. As she waved, the blossoms fell apart and danced a little in the breeze.

Shamli station looked the same as it had the day before. The same train stood at the same platform and the same dogs prowled beside the fence. I waited on the platform till the bell clanged for the train to leave, but Koki did not come.

Somehow, I was not disappointed. I had never really expected her to come.

Shamli would always be there. And I could always come back, looking for Major Roberts.

My Most Important Day

ONE SUMMER MORNING I was up a little earlier than usual, well before sunrise, well before my buxom landlady, Bibiji, called up to me to come down for my tea and parantha. It was going to be a special day and I wanted to tell the world about it. But when you're just twenty-four the world isn't really listening to you.

I bathed at the tap, put on a clean (but unironed) shirt, trousers that needed cleaning, shoes that needed polishing. I never cared much about appearances. But I did have a nice leather belt with studs! I tightened it to the last rung. I was slim, just a little undernourished.

On the streets, the milkmen on their bicycles were making their rounds, reminding me of William Saroyan, who sold newspapers as a boy, and recounted his experiences in *The Bicycle Rider in Beverley Hills*. Stray dogs and cows were nosing at dustbins. A truck loaded with bananas was slowly making its way towards the mandi. In the distance there was the whistle of an approaching train.

One or two small tea shops had just opened, and I stopped at one of them for a cup of tea. As it was a special day, I decided to treat myself to an omelette. The shopkeeper placed a record on his new electric record player, and the strains of a popular film tune served to wake up all the neighbours—a song about a girl's red dupatta being blown away by a gust of wind and then being retrieved by a handsome but unemployed youth. I finished my omelette and set off down the road to the bazaar.

It was a little too early for most of the shops to be open, but the news agency would be the first and that was where I was heading.

And there it was: the National News Agency, with piles of fresh newspapers piled up at the entrance. The *Leader* of Allahabad, the *Pioneer* of Lucknow, the *Tribune* of Ambala, and the bigger national dailies. But where was the latest *Illustrated Weekly of India*? Was it late this week? I did not always get up at six in the morning to pick up the *Weekly*, but this week's issue was a special one. It was my issue, my special bow to the readers of India and the whole wide beautiful wonderful world. My novel was to be published in England, but first it would be serialized in India!

Mr Gupta popped his head out of the half-open shop door and smiled at me.

'What brings you here so early this morning?'

'Has the *Weekly* arrived?'

'Come in. It's here. I can't leave it on the pavement.'

I produced a rupee. 'Give me two copies.'

'Something special in it? Did you win first prize in the crossword competition?'

My hands were not exactly trembling as I opened the magazine, but my heart was in my mouth as I flipped through the pages of that revered journal—the one and only family magazine of the 1950s, the gateway to literary success—edited by a quirky Irishman, Shaun Mandy.

And there it was: the first instalment of my novel, that naïve, youthful novel on which I had toiled for so long. It had lively, evocative illustrations by Mario, who wasn't much older than me. And a picture of the young author, looking gauche and gaunt and far from intellectual.

I waved the magazine in front of Mr Gupta. 'My novel!' I told him. 'In this and the next five issues!'

He wasn't too impressed. 'Well, I hope circulation won't drop,' he said. 'And you should have sent them a better photograph.'

Expansively, I bought a third copy.

'Circulation is going up!' said Mr Gupta with a smile.

The bazaar was slowly coming to life. Spring was

in the air, and there was a spring in my step as I
sauntered down the road. I wanted to tell the world
about my triumph, but was the world interested? I
had no mentors in our sleepy little town. There was
no one to whom I could go and confide: 'Look what
I've done. And it was all due to your encouragement,
thanks!' Because there really hadn't been anyone to
encourage or help, not then nor in the receding past.
Devinder had left Dehra shortly after my return, for
he had gone to Delhi to get some kind of employment.
My other friends—Somi, Ranbir and Kishen—too
weren't here in Dehra. Had they been with me, they
would have gone around announcing my achievement
to everyone in town. The members of the local cricket
team, to which I belonged, would certainly be
interested, and one or two would exclaim: 'Shabash!
Now you can get us some new pads and a set of balls!'
And there were other friends who would demand a
party at the chaat shop, which was fine, but would
any of them read my book? Readers were not exactly
thick on the ground, even in those pre-television, pre-
computer days. But perhaps one or two would read it,
out of loyalty.

A cow stood in the middle of the road, blocking
my way.

'See here, friend cow,' I said, displaying the

magazine to the ruminating animal. 'Here's the first instalment of my novel. What do you think of it?'

The cow looked at the magazine with definite interest. Those crisp new pages looked good to eat. She craned forward as if to accept my offer of breakfast, but I snatched the magazine away.

'I'll lend it to you another day,' I said, and moved on.

I got on quite well with cows, especially stray ones. There was one that blocked the steps up to my room, sheltering there at night or when it rained. The cow had become used to me scrambling over her to get to the steps; my comings and goings did not bother her. But she was resentful of people who tried to prod or push her out of the way. To the delight of the other tenants, she had taken a dislike to the *munshi*, the property owner's rent collector, and often chased him away.

I really don't recall how the rest of that day passed, except that late evening, when the celebrations with friends were over, I found myself alone in my little room, trimming my kerosene lamp. It was too early to sleep, and I'd done enough walking that day. So I pulled out my writing pad and began a new story. I knew even then that the first wasn't going to be enough. Sheherzade had to keep telling stories in order to put off her execution. I would have to keep writing them in order to keep that *munshi* at bay and put off my eviction.

A Handful of Nuts

1

IT WASN'T THE room on the roof, but a large room with a balcony in front and a small veranda at the back. On the first floor of an old shopping complex, still known as Astley Hall, it faced the town's main road, although a walled-in driveway separated it from the street pavement. A neem tree grew in front of the building, and during the early rains, when the neem-pods fell and were crushed underfoot, they gave off a rich, pungent odour which I can never forget.

I had taken the room at the very modest rent of thirty-five rupees a month, payable in advance to the stout Punjabi widow who ran the provisions store downstairs. Her provisions ran to rice, lentils, spices and condiments, but I wasn't doing any cooking then, there wasn't time, so for a quick snack I'd cross the road and consume a couple of samosas or vegetable patties. Whenever I received a decent fee for a story,

I'd treat myself to some sliced ham and a loaf of bread, and make myself ham sandwiches. If any of my friends were around, like Peter or Anand, they'd make short work of the ham sandwiches.

I don't think I ever went hungry, but I was certainly underweight and undernourished, eating irregularly in cheap restaurants and dhabas and suffering frequent stomach upheavals. The years I spent abroad had done nothing to improve my constitution, as there, too, I had lived largely on what was sold over the counter in snack-bars—baked beans on toast being the standard fare.

At the corner of the block, near the Orient Cinema, was a little restaurant called Komal's, run by a rotund Sikh gentleman who seldom left his seat near the window. Here I had a reasonably good lunch of dal, rice and a vegetable curry, for two or three rupees.

There were a few other regulars—a college teacher, a couple of salesmen, and occasionally someone waiting for a film show to begin. Peter and Anand did not trail me to this place, as it was a little lowbrow for them (Peter being Swiss and Anand being from Doon School); nor was it frequented much by students or children. It was lower middle-class, really; professional men who were still single and forced to eat in the town came here. I wasn't bothered by anyone here. And it suited me in other ways, because there was a news-stand close by and I could buy a paper or a magazine and skim through it before or after my meal. Determined as I was to make a living by writing, I had made it my duty to study every English language publication that found its way to Dehra (most of them did), to see which of them published short fiction. A surprisingly large number of magazines did publish short stories; the trouble was, the rates of payment were not very high, the average being about twenty-five rupees a story.

Ten stories a month would therefore fetch me two hundred and fifty rupees—just enough for me to get by!

After eating at Komal's, I'd make my way to the up-market Indiana for a cup of coffee, which was all I could afford there. Indiana was for the smart set. In the evenings it boasted a three-piece band, and you could dance if you had a partner, although dancing cheek to cheek went out with the Second World War. From noon to three, Larry Gomes, a Dehra boy of Goan origin, tinkled on the piano, playing old favourites or new hits.

That spring morning, only one or two tables were occupied—by business people, who weren't listening to the music, so Larry went through a couple of old numbers for my benefit, *September Song* and *I'll See You Again*. At twenty-four, I was very old-fashioned.

Larry received three hundred rupees a month and a free lunch, so he was slightly better off than me. Also, his father owned a small music and record shop a short distance away.

While I was sipping my coffee and pondering upon my financial affairs (which were non-existent, as I had no finances), in walked the rich and baggy-eyed Maharani of Magador with her daughter Indu. I stood up to greet her and she gave me a gracious smile.

She knew that some years previously, I had been infatuated with her daughter. She had even intercepted one of my love letters, but she had been quite sporting about it, and had told me that I wrote a nice letter. Now she knew that I was writing stories for magazines, and she said, 'We read your story in the *Weekly* last week. It was quite charming, didn't I say you'd make a good writer?' I blushed and thanked her, while Indu gave me a mischievous smile. She was still at college.

'You must come and see us someday,' said the Maharani and moved on majestically. Indu, small-boned and petite and dressed in something blue, looked more than ever like a butterfly; soft, delicate, flitting away just as you thought you could touch her.

They sat at a table in a corner, and I returned to contemplate the coffee-stains on the table-cloth for, I had, of course, splashed my coffee all over the place.

Larry had observed my confusion, and guessing its

cause, now played a very old tune which only Indu's mother would have recognized: *'I kiss your little hands, madame, I long to kiss your lips . . .'*

On my way out, Larry caught my eye and winked at me.

'Next time I'll give you a tip,' I said.

'Save it for the waiter,' said Larry.

It was hot in the April sunshine, and I headed for my room, wishing I had a fan.

Stripping to vest and underwear, I lay down on the bed and stared at the ceiling. The ceiling stared back at me. I turned on my side and looked across the balcony, at the leaves of the neem tree. They were absolutely still. There was not even the promise of a breeze.

I dozed off, and dreamt of my princess, her deep dark eyes and the tint of winter moonlight on her cheeks. I opened my eyes to find Sitaram, the washerman's son, sitting at the foot of my bed.

Sitaram must have been about sixteen, a skinny boy with large hands, large feet and large ears. He had loose sensual lips. An unprepossessing youth, whom I found irritating in the extreme; but as he lived with his parents in the quarters behind the flat, there was no avoiding him.

'How did you get in here?' I asked brusquely.

'The door was open.'

'That doesn't mean you can walk right in. What do you want?'

'Don't you have any clothes for washing? My father asked.'

'I wash my own clothes.'

'And sheets?' He studied the sheet I was lying on. 'Don't you wash your sheet? It is very dirty.'

'Well, it's the only one I've got. So buzz off.'

But he was already pulling the sheet out from under me. 'I'll wash it for you free. You are a nice man. My mother says you are *seedha-saada*, very innocent.'

'I am not innocent. And I need the sheet.'

'I will bring you another. I will lend it to you free. We get lots of sheets to wash. Yesterday six sheets came from the hospital. Some people were killed in a bus accident.'

'You mean the sheets came from the morgue—they were used to cover dead bodies? I don't want a sheet from the morgue.'

'But it is very clean. You know *khatmals* (bedbugs) can't live on dead bodies. They like fresh blood.'

He went away with my sheet and came back five minutes later with a freshly-ironed, clean bedsheet.

'Don't worry,' he said. 'It's not from the hospital.'

'Where is this one from?'

'Indiana Hotel. I will give them a hospital sheet in exchange.'

2

The gardens were bathed in moonlight, as I walked down the narrow old roads of Dehra—I stopped near the Maharani's house and looked over the low wall. The lights were still on in some of the rooms. I waited for some time until I saw Indu come to a window. She had a book in her hand, so I guessed she'd been reading. Maybe if I sent her a poem, she'd read it. A poem about a small red virgin rose.

But it wouldn't bring me any money.

I walked back to the bazaar, to the bright lights of the cinemas and small eating houses. It was only eight o'clock. The street was still crowded. Nowadays it's traffic; then it was just full of people. And so you were constantly bumping into people you knew—or did not know . . .

I was staring at a poster of Nimmi, sexiest of Indian actresses, when a hand descended on my shoulder, and I turned to see Anand, the genius from Doon School, whose father owned the New Empire cinema.

'Jalebis, Rusty, jalebis,' he crooned. Although he was from a rich family, he never seemed to have any pocket-money. And of course it's easier to borrow from a poor man than it is to borrow from a rich one! Why is that, I wonder? There was Peter, for instance, who lived in a posh boarding-house, but was always cadging small sums off me—to pay his laundry bill or assist in his consumption of Charminar cigarettes: without them he was a nervous wreck. And with Anand it was jalebis . . .

'I haven't had a cheque for weeks,' I told him.

'What about the story you were writing for the BBC?'

'Well, I've just sent it to them.'

'And the novel you were writing?'

'I'm still writing it.'

'Jalebis will cost only two rupees.'

'Oh, all right . . .'

Anand stuffed himself with jalebis while I contented myself with a samosa. Anand wished to be an artist, poet and diarist, somewhat in the manner of Andre Gide, and had even given me a copy of Gide's *Fruits of the Earth* in an endeavour to influence me in the same direction. It is still with me today, fifty years later, his spidery writing scrawling a message across the dancing angel drawn on the title-page. Our favourite books outlast our dreams . . .

Of course, after the jalebis I had to see Anand home. If I hadn't met him that day, someone else would have had to walk home with him. He was terrified of walking down the narrow lane to his house once darkness had fallen. There were no lights and the overhanging mango, neem and peepal trees made it a place of Stygian gloom. It was said that a woman had hanged herself from a mango tree on this very lane, and Anand was always in a dither lest he should see the lady dangling in front of him.

He kept a small pocket torch handy, but after leaving him at his gate I would have to return sans torch, for nothing could persuade him to part with it. On the way back, I would bump into other pedestrians who would be stumbling along the lane, guided by slivers of moonlight or the pale glimmer from someone's window.

Only the blind man carried a lamp.

'And what need have you of a light?' we asked.

'So that fools do not stumble against me in the dark.'

But I did not care for torchlight. I had taught myself to use whatever the night offered—moonlight, full and partial; starlight; the light from street lamps, from windows, from half-open doors. The night is beautiful, made ugly only by the searing headlights of cars.

When I got back to my room, the shops had closed and only the lights in Sitaram's quarters were on. His parents were quarrelling, and the entire neighbourhood could hear them. It was always like that. The husband was drunk and abusive; she refused to open the door for him, told him to go and sleep elsewhere. After some time he retreated into the dark.

I had no lights, as my landlady had neglected to pay the electricity bill for the past six months. But I did not mind the absence of light, although at times I would have liked an electric fan.

It meant, of course, that I could not type or even write by hand except when the full moon poured over the balcony. But I could always manage a few lines of poetry on a large white sheet of paper.

This sheet of paper is my garden,
These words my flowers.
I do not ask a miracle this night,
Other than you beside me in the bright moonlight.

And there I got stuck. The last lines always fox me, one reason why I never became a poet, I guess.

'And we cling to each other for a long, long time . . .' Shades of *September Song?*

In any case, I couldn't send it to Indu, as her mother would be sure to intercept the letter and read it first. The idea of her daughter clinging to me like a vine would not have appealed to the Maharani.

I would have to think of a more mundane method of making my feelings known.

3

There was some excitement, as Stewart Granger, the British film actor, was in town.

Stewart Granger in Dehra? Occasionally, a Bombay film star passed through, but this was the first time we were going to see a foreign star. We all knew what he looked like, of course. The Odeon and Orient cinemas had been showing British and American films since the days of the silent movies. Occasionally, they still showed 'silents', as their sound systems were antiquated and the projectors rattled a good deal, drowning the dialogue. This did not matter if the star was John Wayne (or even Stewart Granger) as their lines were quite predictable, but it made a difference if you were trying to listen to Nelson Eddy sing *At the Balalaika* or Hope and Crosby exchanging wisecracks.

We had assembled outside the Indiana and were discussing the phenomenon of having Stewart Granger in town. What was he doing here?

'Making a film, I suppose,' I ventured.

Mohan, the lawyer, demurred, 'What about? Nobody's written a book about Dehra, except you, Rusty, and no one has read yours. Has someone bought the film rights?'

'No such luck. And besides, my hero is eighteen and Stewart Granger is thirty-six.'

'Doesn't matter. They'll change the story.'

'Not if I can help it.'

Peter had another theory.

'He's visiting his old aunt in Rajpur.'

'We never knew he had an aunt in Rajpur.'

'Nor did I. It's just a theory.'

'You and your theories. We'll ask the owner of Indiana. Stewart Granger is going to stay here, isn't he?'

Mr Kapoor of Indiana enlightened us. 'They're location-hunting for a shikar movie. It's called *Harry Black and the Tiger.*'

'Stewart Granger is playing a black man?' asked Peter.

'No, no, that's an English surname.'

'English is a funny language,' said Peter, who believed in the superiority of the French tongue.

'We don't have any tigers left in these forests,' I said.

'They'll bring in a circus tiger and let it loose,' said Mohan.

'In the jungle, I hope,' said Peter. 'Or will they let it loose on Rajpur Road?'

'Preferably in the Town Hall,' said Mohan, who was having some trouble with the municipality over his house tax.

Stewart Granger did not disappoint.

At about two in the afternoon, the hottest part of the day, he arrived in an open Ford convertible, shirtless and vestless. He was in his prime then, in pretty good condition after playing opposite Ava Gardner in *Bhowani Junction*, and everyone remarked on his fine torso and general good looks. He made himself comfortable in a cool corner of the Indiana and proceeded to down several bottles of chilled beer, much to everyone's admiration. Larry Gomes, at the piano, started playing *Sweet Rosie o' Grady* until Granger, who wasn't Irish, stopped him and asked for something more modern. Larry obliged with *Goodnight Irene*, and Stewart, now into his third bottle of beer, began singing the refrain. At the next table, Peter, Mohan and I, trying to keep pace with the star's consumption of beer, joined in the chorus, and before long there was a mad sing-song in the restaurant.

The editor of the local paper, the *Doon Chronicle*, tried interviewing the star, but made little progress. Someone gave him an information and publicity sheet which did the rounds. It said Stewart Granger was born in 1913, and that he had black hair and brown eyes. He still had them—unless the hair was a toupe. It said his height was 6 feet 2 inches, and that he weighed 196 lbs. He looked every pound of it. It also said his youthful ambition was to become a 'nerve specialist'. We looked at him with renewed respect, although none of us was quite sure what a 'nerve specialist' was supposed to do.

'We just get on your nerves,' said Mr Granger when asked, and everyone laughed.

He tucked into his curry and rice with relish, downed another beer, and returned to his waiting car. A few good-natured jests, a wave and a smile, and the star and his entourage drove off into the foothills.

We heard, later, that they had decided to make the film in Mysore, in distant south India. No wonder it turned out to be a flop.

Two months later, Yul Brynner passed through but he didn't cause the same excitement. We were getting used to film stars. His film wasn't made in Dehra, either. They did it in Spain. Another flop.

4

Why have I chosen to write about the twenty-fourth year of my life?

Well, for one thing, it's often one of the most significant years in any young person's life. A time for falling in love; a time to set about making your dreams come true; a time to venture forth, to blaze new trails, take risks, do your own thing, follow your star . . . And so it was with me.

I was just back after four years of living in the West; I had found a publisher in London for my first novel; I was looking for fresh fields and new laurels; and I wanted to prove that I could succeed as a writer with my small hometown in India as a base, without having to live in London or Paris or New York.

In a couple of weeks' time it would be my twenty-fifth birthday, and I was feeling good about it.

I had mentioned the date to someone—Mohan, I think—and before long I was being told by everyone I knew that I would have to celebrate the event in a big way, twenty-five being an age of great significance in a young man's life. To tell the truth I wasn't feeling very youthful. The Komal restaurant's rich food, swimming in oil, was beginning to take its toll, and I spent a lot of time turning input into output, so to speak.

Finding me flat on my back, Sitaram sat down beside me on my bed and expressed his concern for my health. I was too weak to drive him away.

'Just a stomach upset,' I said. 'It will pass off. You can go.'

'I will bring you some curds—very good for the stomach when you have the *dast*—when you are in full flow.'

'I took some tablets.'

'Medicine no good. Take curds.'

Seeing that he was serious, I gave him two rupees and he went off somewhere and returned after ten minutes with a bowl of curd. I found it quite refreshing, and he promised to bring more that evening. Then he said: 'So you will be twenty-five soon. A big party.'

'How did you know?' I asked, for I certainly hadn't mentioned it to him.

'Sitaram knows everything!'

'How did you find out?'

'I heard them talking in the Indiana, as I collected the table-cloths for washing. Will you have the party in Indiana?'

'No, no, I can't afford it.'

'Have it here then. I will help you.'

'Let's see . . .'

'How many people will you call for the tea-party?'

'I don't know. Most of them are demanding beer—it's expensive.'

'Give them *kachi*, they make it in our village behind the police lines. I'll bring a jerry-can for you. It's very cheap and very strong. Big *nasha* (intoxication)!'

'How do you know? Do you drink it?'

'I never drink. My father drinks enough for everyone.'

'Well, I can't give it to my guests.'

'Who will come?'

I gave some consideration to my potential guest list. There'd be Anand demanding jalebis and beer, a sickening combination! And Peter wanting French toast, I supposed. (Was French toast eaten by the French? It seemed very English, somehow.) And Mohan wanting something stronger than beer. (After two whiskys, he claimed that he had discovered the fourth dimension.) And there were my young Sikh friends from the Dilaram Bazaar, who would be happy with lots to eat. And perhaps Larry Gomes would drop in.

Dare I invite the Maharani and Indu? Would they fit in with the rest of the mob? Perhaps I could invite them to a separate tea-party at the Indiana. Cream-rolls and cucumber sandwiches.

And where would the money come from for all these celebrations? My bank balance stood at a little over three hundred rupees—enough to pay the rent and the food bill at Komal's and make myself a new pair of trousers. The pair I'd bought on the Mile End Road in London, two years previously, were now very baggy and had a shine on the seat. The other pair, made of non-shrink material, got smaller at every wash; I had given them to a tailor to turn into a pair of shorts.

Sitaram, of course, was willing to lend me any number of trousers provided I wasn't fussy about who the owners were, and gave them back in time for them to be washed and ironed again before being delivered to their rightful owners. I did, on an occasion, borrow a pair made of a nice checked material, and was standing outside the Indiana, chatting to the owner, when I realized that he was staring hard at the trousers.

'I have a pair just like yours,' he remarked.

'It shows you have good taste,' I said, and gave Sitaram an earful when I got back to the flat.

'I can't trust you with other people's trousers!' I shouted. 'Couldn't you have lent me a pair belonging to someone who lives far from here?'

He was genuinely contrite. 'I was looking for the right size,' he said. 'Would you like to try a dhoti? You will look good in a dhoti. Or a lungi. There's a purple lungi here, it belongs to a sub-inspector of police.'

'A purple lungi? The police are human, after all.'

Money talks—and it's usually saying goodbye.

A freelance writer can't tell what he's going to make from one month to the next. This uncertainty is part of the charm of the writing life, but it can also make for some nail-biting finishes when it comes to paying the rent, the food bill at Komal's, postage on my articles and correspondence, typing paper, toothpaste, socks, shaving soap, candles (there was no light in my room) and other necessities. And friends like Peter and Mohan (the only out-of-work lawyer I have ever known) did not make it any easier for me.

Peter, though Swiss, had served in the French Foreign Legion, and had been on the run in Vietnam along with the French administration and army once the Vietnamese had decided they'd had enough of the *Marseillaise*. The French are not known for their military prowess, although they would like to think otherwise.

Peter had drifted into Dehra as the assistant to a German newspaper correspondent, Von Radloff, who based his dispatches on the Indian papers and sent them out with a New Delhi dateline. Dehra was a little cooler than Delhi, and it was still pretty in parts. You could lead a pleasant life there, it was still easier if you had an income.

Peter and Radloff fell out, and Peter decided he'd set up on his own as a correspondent. But there weren't many takers for his articles in Europe, and his debts were mounting. He continued to live in an expensive guest house whose owner, an unusually tolerant landlord, reminded him one day that he was five months in arrears.

Peter took to turning up at my room around the same time as the postman, to see if I'd received any cheques or international money orders.

'Only pounds,' I told him one day. 'No French or

Swiss francs. How could I possibly aspire to a French publisher?'

'Pounds will do. I owe my Sardarji about five thousand rupees.'

'Well, you'll have to keep owing him. My twelve pounds from the *Young Elizabethan* won't do much for you.'

The *Young Elizabethan* was a classy British children's magazine, edited by Kaye Webb and Pat Campbell. A number of my early stories found a home between its covers. Alas, like many other good things, it vanished a couple of years later. But in that golden year of my debut it was one of my mainstays.

'Why don't you look for cheaper accommodation?' I asked Peter.

'I have to keep up appearances. How can the correspondent of the Franco-German press live in a hovel like yours?'

'Well, suit yourself,' I said. 'I hope you get some money soon.' All the same, I lent him two hundred rupees, and of course I never saw it again. Would I have enough for my birthday party? That was now the burning question.

5

Early one morning I decided I'd take a long cycle ride out of the town's precincts. I'd read all about the dawn coming up like thunder, but had never really got up early enough to witness it. I asked Sitaram to do me a favour and wake me at six. He woke me at five. It was just getting light. As I dressed, the colour of the sky changed from ultramarine to a clear shade of lavender, and then the sun came up gloriously naked.

I had borrowed a cycle from my landlady—it was occasionally used by her son or servant to deliver purchases to favoured customers—and I rode off down the Rajpur Road in a rather wobbly, zig-zag manner, as it was about five years since I had ridden a cycle. I was careful; I did not want to end up a cripple like Denton Welch, the sensitive author of *A Voice in the Clouds*, whose idyllic country cycle-ride had ended in disaster and tragedy.

Dehra's traffic is horrific today, but there was not much of it then, and at six in the morning the roads were deserted. In any case, I was soon out of the town and then I reached the tea-gardens. I stopped at a small wayside teashop for refreshment and while I was about to dip a hard bun in my tea, a familiar shadow fell across the table, and I looked up to see Sitaram grinning at me. I'd forgotten—he too had a cycle.

Dear friend and familiar! I did not know whether to be pleased or angry.

'My cycle is faster than yours,' he said.

'Well, then carry on riding it to Rishikesh. I'll try to keep up with you.'

He laughed. 'You can't escape me that way, writer-sahib. I'm hungry.'

'Have something, then.'

'We will practise for your birthday.' And he helped himself to a boiled egg, two buns, and a sponge cake that looked as though it had been in the shop for a couple of years. If Sitaram can digest that, I thought, then he's a true survivor.

'Where are you going?' he asked, as I prepared to mount my cycle.

'Anywhere,' I said. 'As far as I feel like going.'

'Come, I will show you roads that you have never seen before.'

Were these prophetic words? Was I to discover new paths and new meanings courtesy of the washerman's son?

'Lead on, light of my life,' I said, and he beamed and set off at a good speed so that I had trouble keeping up with him. He left the main road, and took a bumpy, dusty path through a bamboo grove. It was a fairly broad path and we could cycle side by side. It led out of the bamboo grove into an extensive tea-garden, then turned and twisted before petering out beside a small canal.

We rested our cycles against the trunk of a mango

tree, and as we did so, a flock of green parrots, disturbed by our presence, flew out from the tree, circling the area and making a good deal of noise. In India, the land of the loudspeaker, even the birds have learnt to shout in order to be heard.

The parrots finally settled on another tree. The mangoes were beginning to form, but many would be bruised by the birds before they could fully ripen.

A kingfisher dived low over the canal and came up with a gleaming little fish.

'Too tiny for us,' I said, 'or we might have caught a few.'

'We'll eat fish tikkas in the bazaar on our way back,' said Sitaram, a pragmatic person.

While Sitaram went exploring the canal banks, I sat down and rested my back against the bole of the mango tree.

A sensation of great peace stole over me. I felt in complete harmony with my surroundings—the gurgle of the canal water, the trees, the parrots, the bark of the tree, the warmth of the sun, the softness of the faint breeze, the caterpillar on the grass near my feet, the grass itself, each blade . . . And I knew that if I always remained close to these things, growing things, the natural world, life would come alive for me, and I would be able to write as long as I lived.

Optimism surged through me, and I began singing

an old song of Nelson Eddy's, a Vincent Huyman composition—

When you are down and out,
Lift up your head and shout—
It's going to be a great day!

Across the canal, moving through some wild babul trees, a dim figure seemed to be approaching. It wasn't the boy, it wasn't a stranger, it was someone I knew. Though he remained dim, I was soon able to recognize my father's face and form.

He stood there, smiling, and the song died on my lips.

But perhaps it was the song that had brought him back for a few seconds. He had always liked Nelson Eddy, collected his records. Where were they now? Where were the songs of old? The past has served us well; we must preserve all that was good in it.

As I stood up and raised my hand in greeting, the figure faded away.

My dear, dear father. How much I had loved him. And I had been only eleven when he had been snatched away. Off and on he had given me some sign that he was still with me, would always be with me . . .

There was a great splashing close by, and I looked down to see that Sitaram was in the water. I hadn't even noticed him slip off his clothes and jump into the canal.

He beckoned to me to join him, and after a moment's hesitation, I decided to do so. Sitaram and I romped around in the waist-deep water for quite some time. After a while I climbed the opposite bank and walked to the place where I had seen my father approaching. But there was no sign that anyone had been there. Not even a footprint.

6

It was mid-afternoon when we cycled back to the town. Siesta-time for many, but some brave souls were playing cricket in a vacant lot. There were spacious bungalows in the Dalanwala area; they had lawns and well-kept gardens. Dehra's establishment lived here. As did the Maharani of Magador, whose name-plate caught my eye as we rode slowly past the gate. I got off my cycle and stood at the kerb, looking over the garden wall.

'What are you looking at?' asked Sitaram, dismounting beside me.

'I want to invite the Maharani's daughter to my birthday party. But I don't suppose her mother will allow her to come.'

'Invite the mother too,' said Sitaram.

'Brilliant!' I said. 'Hit two Ranis with one stone.'

'Two birds in hand!' added Sitaram, who remembered his English proverbs from Class Seven. 'And look, there is one of them in the bushes now!'

He pointed towards a hedge of hibiscus, where Indu was at work pruning the branches. Our voices had carried across the garden, and she looked up and stared at us for a few seconds before recognizing me. She walked slowly across the grass and stopped on the other side of the low wall, smiling faintly, looking from me to Sitaram and back to me.

'Hello,' she said. 'Where have you been cycling?'

'Oh, all over the place. Across the canal and into the fields like Hemingway. Now we're on our way home. Sitaram lives next door to me. When I saw your place, I thought I'd stop and say hello. Is your mother at home?'

'Yes, she's resting. Do you want to see her?'

'Er, no. Well, sure, but I won't disturb her. What I wanted to say was—if you're free on the 19th, come and join me and my friends for tea. It's my birthday, my twenty-fifth.'

'How nice. But my mother won't let me go alone.'

'The invitation includes her. If she comes, will you?'

'I'll ask her.'

I looked into her eyes. Deep brown, rather mischievous eyes. Were they responding to my look of gentle adoration? Or were they just amused because I was so self-conscious, so gauche? I could write stories, earn a living, converse with people from all walks of life, ride a bicycle, play football, climb trees, put back a few drinks, walk for miles without tiring, play with babies, charm grandmothers, impress fathers; but when it came to making an impression on the opposite sex, I was sadly out of depth, a complete dunce. It was I, not Indu, who had to hide the blushes . . .

My intentions towards Indu were perfectly honourable, although I couldn't see her mother accepting me into the royal fold. But perhaps one day when fame and fortune were mine (soon, I hoped!) Indu would give up her protected existence and come and live with me in a house by the sea or a villa on some tropical isle.

As Indu gazed into my eyes, I said, quite boldly and to my own surprise, 'I have to kiss you one of these days, Indu.'

'Why not today?'

She was offering me her cheek, and that's where I started, but then she let me kiss her on her lips, and it was so sweet and intoxicating that when I felt someone pressing my hand I was sure it was Indu. I returned the pressure, then realized that Indu was on the other side of the wall, still holding the hedge-cutters. I'd quite forgotten Sitaram's presence. The pressure of his hand increased; I turned to look at him and he nodded approvingly. Indu had drawn away from the wall just as her mother's voice carried to us across the garden: 'Who are you talking to, Indu? Is it someone we know?'

'Just a college student!' Indu called back, and then, waving, walked slowly in the direction of the veranda. She turned once and said, 'I'll come to the party, Mother too!'

And I was left with Sitaram holding my hand.

'Only one thing missing,' he said.

'What's that?'

'*Filmi* music.'

There was *filmi* music in full measure when we got to the Orient cinema, where they were showing *Mr and Mrs 55* starring Madhubala, who was everybody's heart-throb that year. Sitaram insisted that I return my bicycle and join him in the cheap seats, which I did, almost passing out from the aromatic *beedi* smoke that filled the hall. The Orient had once shown English films, and I remembered seeing an early British comedy, *The Ghost of St. Michael's* (with Will Hay), when I was a boy. The front of the cinema, facing the parade-ground, was decorated with a bas-relief of dancers, designed by Sudhir Khastgir, art master at the

Doon School, and the decorations certainly lent character to the building—the rest of its character was fast disintegrating. But I enjoyed watching the crowd at the cinema. For me, the audience was always more interesting than the performers.

All I remember of the film was that Sitaram got very restless whenever Madhubala appeared on the screen. He would whistle along with the tongawallahs and squeeze my arm to indicate that he was really turned on by his favourite screen heroine. A good thing Madhubala wasn't coming to town, or there'd have been a riot; but for some time there had been a rumour that Prem Nath, a successful male star, would be visiting Dehra, and my landlady had been quite excited at the prospect. But Sitaram was not turned on by Prem Nath. It was Madhubala or nothing.

After the film, while wending our way through the bazaar, we were accosted by Anand, who walked with us to the Frontier Sweet Shop, where fresh hot jalebis were being dished out to the evening's first customers.

'Your turn to pay,' I said.

'Next time, next time,' promised the pride of the Doon School.

'I'm broke,' I said.

'Your friend must have some money.'

It turned out that Sitaram did possess a few

crumpled notes, which he thrust into my hand.

'What does your friend do?' asked Anand.

'He's in the garment business,' I said.

Anand looked at Sitaram with renewed respect. When he'd had his fill of jalebis he insisted on showing us his new painting. So we walked home with him along his haunted alley, and he took us into his studio and proudly displayed a painting of a purple lady, very long in the arms and legs, and somewhat flat-chested.

'Well, what do you think?' asked Anand, standing back and looking at his bizarre creation with an affectionate eye.

'Are you doing it for your school founder's day?' I asked innocently.

'No, nudes aren't permitted. But you should see my study of angels in flight. It won the first prize!'

'Well, if you give this one a halo and wings, it could be an angel.'

Anand turned from me in disgust and asked Sitaram for his opinion.

Sitaram stared at the painting quizzically and said, 'She must have given all her clothes for washing.'

'There speaks the garment manufacturer,' I put in.

Anand saw us to the door, but not down the dark alley; he never took it alone. All his life he was to be afraid of being alone in the dark. Well, we all have our phobias. To this day, I won't use a lift or escalator unless I have company.

Sitaram and I walked back quite comfortably in the dark. He linked his fingers with mine and broke into song, a little off-key; he was no Saigal or Rafi. We cut across the maidan, and a quarter-moon kept us company. I was overcome by a feeling of tranquillity, a love for all the world, and wondered if it had something to do with the vision of my father earlier in the day.

As we climbed the steps to the landing that separated my rooms from Sitaram's quarters, we could hear his parents' voices raised in their nightly recriminations. His mother was a virago, no doubt; and his father was a drunk who gambled away most of his earnings. For Sitaram it was a trap from which there was only one escape. And he voiced my thought.

'I'll leave home one of these days,' he said.

'Well, tonight you can stay with me.'

I'd said it without any forethought, simply on an impulse. He followed me into my room, without bothering to inform his parents that he was back.

My landlady's large double-bed provided plenty of space for both of us. She hadn't used it since her husband's death, some six or seven years previously. And it was unlikely that she would be using it again.

7

Someone was getting married, and the wedding band, brought up on military marches, unwittingly broke into the *Funeral March*. And they played loud enough to wake the dead.

After a medley of Souza marches, they switched to Hindi film tunes, and Sitaram came in, flung his arms around, and shattered my ear-drums with Talat Mehmood's latest love ballad. I responded with the *Volga Boatmen* in my best Nelson Eddy manner, and my landlady came running out of her shop downstairs wanting to know if the washerman had strangled his wife or vice-versa.

Anyway, it was to be a week of celebrations . . .

When I opened my eyes next day, it was to find a bright red geranium staring me in the face, accompanied by the aromatic odour of a crushed geranium leaf. Sitaram was thrusting a potted geranium at me and wishing me a happy birthday. I brushed a caterpillar from my pillow and sat up. Wordsworthian though I was in principle, I wasn't prepared for nature red in tooth and claw.

I picked up the caterpillar on its leaf and dropped it outside.

'Come back when you're a butterfly,' I said.

Sitaram had taken his morning bath and looked

very fresh and spry. Unfortunately, he had doused his head with some jasmine-scented hair oil, and the room was reeking of it. Already a bee was buzzing around him.

'Thank you for the present,' I said. 'I've always wanted a geranium.'

'I wanted to bring a rose-bush but the pot was too heavy.'

'Never mind, geraniums do better on verandas.'

I placed the pot in a sunny corner of the small balcony, and it certainly did something for the place. There's nothing like a red geranium for bringing a balcony to life.

While we were about to plan the day's festivities, a stranger walked through my open door (one day, I'd have to shut it), and declared himself the inventor of a new flush-toilet which, he said, would revolutionize the sanitary habits of the town. We were still living in the thunderbox era, and only the very rich could afford western-style lavatories. My visitor showed me diagrams of a seat which, he said, combined the best of East and West. You could squat on it, Indian-style, without putting too much strain on your abdominal muscles, and if you used water to wash your bottom, there was a little sprinkler attached which, correctly aimed, would do that job for you. It was comfortable, efficient, safe. Your effluent would be stored in a little tank, which could be detached when full, and emptied—where? He hadn't got around to that problem as yet, but he assured me that his invention had a great future.

'But why are you telling me all this?' I asked, 'I can't afford a fancy toilet-seat.'

'No, no, I don't expect you to buy one.'

'You mean I should demonstrate?'

'Not at all. But you are a writer, I hear. I want a name for my new toilet-seat. Can you help?'

'Why not call it the Sit-Safe?' I suggested.

'The Sit-Safe! How wonderful. Young Mr Bond, let me show my gratitude with a small present.' And he thrust a ten-rupee note into my hand and left the room before I could protest. 'It's definitely my birthday,' I said. 'Complete strangers walk in and give me money.'

'We can see three films with that,' said Sitaram.

'Or buy three bottles of beer,' I said.

But there were no more windfalls that morning, and I had to go to the old Allahabad Bank—where my grandmother had kept her savings until they had dwindled away—and withdraw one hundred rupees.

'Can you tell me my balance?' I asked Mr Jain, the elderly clerk who knew my grandmother.

'Two hundred and fifty rupees,' he said with a smile. 'Try to save something!'

I emerged into the hot sunshine and stood on the steps of the bank, where I had stood as a small boy some twelve years back, waiting for Granny to finish her work—I think she had been the only one in the family to put some money by for a rainy day—but there had been many rainy days what with all her various fickle relatives always battening off her.

Well, I had no relatives to support, but here was Peter waiting for me under the old peepal tree. His hands were shaking.

'What's wrong?' I asked.

'Haven't had a cigarette for a week. Come on, buy me a packet of Charminars.'

Sitaram went out and bought samosas and jalebis and little cakes with icing made from solidified ghee. I fetched a few bottles of beer, some orangeades and lemonades and a syrupy cold drink called Vimto which was all the rage then. My landlady, hearing that I was throwing a party, sent me pakoras made with green chillies.

The party, when it happened, was something of an anti-climax.

Anand turned up promptly and ate all the jalebis.

Peter arrived with Mohan, finished the beer, and demanded more.

Nobody paid much attention to Sitaram, he seemed

so much at home. Caste didn't count for much in a fairly modern town, as Dehra was in those days. In any case, from the way Sitaram was strutting around, acting as though he owned the place, it was generally presumed that he was the landlady's son. He brought up a second relay of the lady's pakoras, hotter than the first lot, and they arrived just as the Maharani and Indu appeared in the doorway.

'Happy birthday, dear boy,' boomed the Maharani and seized the largest chilli pakora. Indu appeared behind her and gave me a box wrapped in gold and silver cellophane. I put it on my desk and hoped it contained chocolates, not studs and a tie-pin.

The chilli pakoras did not take long to violate the Maharani's taste-buds.

'Water, water!' she cried, and seeing the bathroom door open, made a dash for the tap.

Alas, the bathroom was the least attractive aspect of my flat. It had yet to be equipped with anything resembling the newly-invented Sit-Safe. But the lid of the thunderbox was fortunately down, as this particular safe hadn't been emptied for a couple of days. It was crowned by a rusty old tin mug. On the wall hung a towel that had seen better days. The remnants of a cake of Lifebuoy soap stood near a cracked washbasin. A lonely cockroach gave the Maharani a welcoming genuflection.

Taking all this in at a glance, she backed out, holding her hand to her mouth.

'Try a Vimto,' said Peter, holding out a bottle gone warm and sticky.

'A glass of beer? asked Anand.

The Maharani grabbed a glass of beer and swallowed it in one long gulp. She came up gasping, gave me a reproachful look—as though the chilli pakora had been intended for her—and said, 'Must go now. Just stopped by to greet you. Thank you very much—you must come to Indu's birthday party. *Next* year.'

Next year seemed a long way off.

'Thank you for the present,' I said.

And then they were gone, and I was left to entertain my cronies.

Mohan was demanding something stronger than beer, and as I felt that way myself, we trooped off to the Royal Cafe; all of us, except Sitaram, who had better things to do.

After two rounds of drinks, I'd gone through what remained of my money. And so I left Peter and Mohan to cadge drinks off one of the latter's clients, while I bid Anand goodbye on the edge of the parade-ground. As it was still light, I did not have to see him home.

Some workmen were out on the parade-ground, digging holes for tent-pegs.

Two children were discussing the coming attraction.

'The circus is coming!'

'Is it big?'

'It's the biggest! Tigers, elephants, horses, chimpanzees! Tight-rope walkers, acrobats, strong men . . .'

'Is there a clown?'

'There has to be a clown. How can you have a circus without a clown?'

I hurried home to tell Sitaram about the circus. It would make a change from the cinema. The room had been tidied up, and the Maharani's present stood on my desk, still in its wrapper.

'Let's see what's inside,' I said, tearing open the packet.

It was a small box of nuts—almonds, pistachios, cashew nuts, along with a few dried figs.

'Just a handful of nuts,' said Sitaram, sampling a fig and screwing up his face.

I tried an almond, found it was bitter and spat it out.

'Must have saved them from her wedding day,' said Sitaram.

'Appropriate in a way,' I said. 'Nuts for a bunch of nuts.'

8

Lines written on a hot summer's night:

On hot summer nights I dream
Of you beside me, near a mountain stream
Cool in our bed of ferns we lie,
Lost in our loving, as the world slips by.

I tried to picture Indu in my arms, the two of us watching the moon come over the mountains. But her face kept dissolving and turning into her mother's. This transition from dream to nightmare kept me from sleeping. Sitaram slept peacefully at the edge of the bed, immune to the mosquitoes that came in like squadrons of dive-bombers. It was much too hot for any body contact, but even then, the sheets were soaked with perspiration.

Tired of his parents' quarrels, and his father's constant threat of turning him out if he did not start contributing towards the family's earnings, Sitaram was practically living with me. I had been on my own for the past five years and had grown used to a form of solitary confinement. I don't think I could have shared my life with an intellectual companion. Peter and Anand were stimulating company in the Indiana or Royal Cafe, but I doubt if I would have enjoyed waking up to their argumentative presences first thing every morning. Peter disagreed with everything I wrote or said; I was too sentimental, too whimsical, too descriptive. He was probably right, but I preferred to write in the manner that gave me the maximum amount of enjoyment. There was more give and take with Anand, but I knew he'd be writing a thousand words to my hundred, and this would have been a little disconcerting to a lazy writer.

Sitaram made no demands on my intellect. He left me to my writing-pad and typewriter. As a physical presence, he was acceptable and grew more interesting by the day. He ran small errands for me, accompanied me on the bicycle-rides which often took us past the Maharani's house. And he took an interest in converting the small balcony into a garden—so much so, that my landlady began complaining that water was seeping through the floor and dripping on to the flour sacks in her ration shop.

The red geranium was joined by a cerise one, and I wondered where it had come from, until I heard the Indiana proprietor complaining that one of his pots was missing.

A potted rose-plant, neglected by Mohan (who neglected his clients with much the same single-minded carelessness) was appropriated and saved from a slow and lingering death. Subjected to cigarette butts, the remnants of drinks and half-eaten meals, it looked as though it would never produce a rose. So it made the journey from Mohan's veranda to mine without protest from its owner (since he was oblivious of its presence) and under Sitaram's ministrations, soon perked up and put forth new leaves and a bud.

My landlady had thrown out a wounded succulent, and this too found a home on the balcony, along with a sickly asparagus-fern left with me by Peter.

A plant hospital, no less!

Coming up the steps one evening, I was struck by the sweet smell of *Raat-ki-Rani*, Queen of the Night, and I was puzzled by its presence because I knew there was none growing on our balcony or anywhere else in the vicinity. In front of the building stood a neem tree, and a mango tree, the last survivor of the mango grove that had occupied this area before it was cleared away for a shopping block. There were no shrubs around—they would not have survived the traffic or the press of people. Only potted plants occupied the shopfronts and veranda-spaces. And yet there was that distinct smell of *Raat-ki-Rani*, growing stronger all the time.

Halfway up the steps, I looked up, and saw my father standing at the top of the steps, in the half-light of a neighbouring window. He was looking at me the way he had done that day near the canal—with affection and a smile playing on his lips—and at first I stood still surprised by happiness. Then, waves of love and the old companionship sweeping over me, I advanced up the steps; but when I reached the top, the vision faded and I stood there alone, the sweet smell of *Raat-ki-Rani* still with me, but no one else, no sound but the distant shunting of an engine.

This was the second time I'd seen my father, or rather his apparition, and I did not know if it portended anything, or if it was just that he wanted to see me again, was trying to cross the gulf between our different worlds, the worlds of yesterday, today, and tomorrow.

Alone on the balcony, looking down at the badly-lit street, I indulged in a bout of nostalgia, recalling boyhood days when my father was my only companion—in the RAF tent outside Delhi, with the hot winds of May and June swirling outside; then the cool evening walks in Dehra, with no destination in mind; and earlier, exploring the beach at Jamnagar, picking up and storing away different kinds of seashells.

I still had one with me—a smooth round shell which must have belonged to a periwinkle. I put it to my ear and heard the hum of the ocean, the siren song of the sea. I knew that one day I would have to choose between the sea and the mountains, but for the moment it was this little sub-tropical valley, hot and humid, patiently waiting for the monsoon rains . . .

The mango trees were sweet with blossom. 'My love is like a red, red rose,' sang Robbie Burns, while John

Clare, another poet of the countryside, declared: 'My love is like a bean-field in blossom.' In India, sweethearts used to meet in the mango-groves at blossom time. They don't do that any more. Mango-groves are no longer private places. Better a dark corner of the Indiana, with Larry Gomes playing old melodies on his piano . . .

I walked down to A.N. John's salon for a haircut, but couldn't get anywhere near the entrance. An excited but good-natured crowd had taken up most of the narrow road as well as a resident's front garden.

'What's happening?' I asked a man who was selling candyfloss.

'Dilip Kumar is inside. He's having a haircut.'

Dilip Kumar! The most popular male star of the silver screen!

'But what's he doing in Dehra?' I asked.

The candyfloss-seller looked at me as though I was a cretin. 'I just told you—having a haircut.'

I moved on to where the owner of the bicycle-hire shop was standing. 'What's Dilip Kumar doing in town?' I asked. He shrugged. 'Don't know. Must be something to do with the circus.'

'Is he the ringmaster for the circus?' asked a little boy in a pyjama suit.

'Of course not,' said the pigtailed girl beside him. 'The circus won't be able to pay him enough.'

'Maybe he owns the circus,' said the little boy.

'It belongs to a friend of his,' said a tongawallah with a knowing air. 'He's come for the opening night.'

Whatever the reasons for Dilip Kumar's presence in Dehra, it was agreed by all that he was in A.N. John's, having a haircut. There was only one way out of A.N. John's and that was by the front door. There were a couple of windows on the side, but the crowd had them well covered.

Finally, the star emerged; beaming, waving to people, looking very handsome indeed in a white bush shirt and neatly-ironed silvery grey trousers. There was a nice open look about him. No histrionics. No impatience to get away. He was the ordinary guy who'd made good.

Where was Sitaram? Why wasn't my star-struck friend in the crowd? I found him later, watching the circus tents go up, but by then Dilip Kumar was on his way to Delhi. He hadn't come for the circus at all. He'd been visiting his young friend Nandu Jauhar at the Savoy in neighbouring Mussoorie.

9

The circus opened on time, and the parade-ground became a fairy land of lights and music. This happened only once in every five years when the Great Gemini

Circus came to town. This particular circus toured every town, large and small, throughout the length and breadth of India, so naturally it took some time for it to return to scenes of past triumphs; and by the time it did so, some of the acts had changed, younger performers had taken the place of some of the older ones, and a new generation of horses, tigers and elephants were on display. So, in effect, it was a brand new circus in Dehra, with only a few familiar faces in the ring or on the trapeze.

The senior clown was an old-timer who'd been to Dehra before, and he welcomed the audience with a flattering little speech which was cut short when one of the prancing ponies farted full in his face. Was this accident or design? We in the audience couldn't tell, but we laughed all the same.

A circus does bring all kinds of people together under the one tent-top. The popular stands were of course packed, but the more expensive seats were also occupied. I caught sight of Indu and her mother. They were accompanied by someone who looked like the Prince of Purkazi. I looked again, and came to the conclusion that it was indeed the Prince of Purkazi. A pang of jealousy assailed me. What was the eligible young prince doing in the company of my princess? Why wasn't he playing cricket for India or the minor counties, or preferably on some distant field in East

UP where bottles and orange-peels would be showered down on the players? Could the Maharani be scheming to get him married to her daughter? The dreadful thought crossed my mind.

He was handsome, he was becoming famous, he was royalty. And he probably owned race-horses.

But not the ones in the circus-ring. They looked reasonably well-fed, and they were obedient; but they weren't of racing stock. A gentle canter around the ring had them snorting and heaving at the flanks as though they'd just finished running all the way from Meerut, their last stop.

Dear Hema Mahajan was watching them with her eagle eye. She was just starting out on her campaign for the SPCA, with particular reference to circus animals, and she had her notebook and fountain-pen poised and ready for action. Hema, then in her thirties, had come into prominence after winning a newspaper short story contest, and her articles and middles were now appearing quite regularly in the national press. She knew Peter and disapproved of him, for he was known to move around in a pony trap. She knew Mohan and disapproved of him; he had shot his neighbour's Dobermann for howling beneath his window all night. She disapproved of the Indiana owner for serving up partridges at Christmas. And did she disapprove of me? Not yet. But I could sense her looking my way to see if I was enjoying the show. That would have gone against me. So I pretended to look bored; then turned towards her with a resigned look and threw my arms up in the air in a sort of world-weary gesture. 'I'm here for the same reasons as you,' was what it meant, and I must have succeeded, because she gave me a friendly nod. Quite a decent sort, Hema.

There were several other acquaintances strewn about the audience, including a pale straw-haired boy called Bob Canter, who had managed to secure Dilip Kumar's autograph earlier that day. Bob was the son of American missionaries, but his heart was in Hindi movies and already he was nursing an ambition to be a film star.

Peter and Anand were absent. They felt the circus was just a little below their intellectual brows. Anand said he had a painting to finish, and Peter was writing a long article on one of the country's Five-Year Plans—don't ask me which one . . . At the time a writer named Khushwant Singh was editing a magazine called *Yojana*, which was all about Five-Year Plans, and he had asked Peter to do the article. I'd offered the editor an article on punch and its five ingredients—spirit, lemon or lime juice, spice, sugar and rose water—but had been politely turned down. Mr Singh liked his Scotch, but punch was not within the purview of the Five-Year Plan.

To return to the circus . . . The trapeze artistes (from Kerala) were very good. The girl on the tight rope (from Andhra) was scintillating in her skin-tight, blue-sequinned costume. The lady lion-tamer (from Tamil Nadu) was daunting, although her lion did look a bit scruffy. The talent seemed to come largely from the south, so that it did not surprise me when the band broke into that lovely Strauss waltz, *Roses of the South*.

The ringmaster came from Bengal. He had a snappy whip, and its sound, as it whistled through the air, was sufficient to command obedience from snarling tigers, prancing ponies, and dancing bears. He did not actually touch anyone with it. The whistle of the whip was sufficient.

Sitaram, who sat beside me looking like Sabu in *The Thief of Baghdad*, was enthralled by all he saw. This was his first circus, and every single act and individual performance had his complete attention. His face was suffused with delighted anticipation. He gasped when the trapeze artistes flew through the air. He laughed at the clown's antics. He sang to the tunes the band played, and he whistled (along with the rowdier sections of the audience) when those alluring southern beauties stood upright on their cantering, wheeling ponies.

'I like the one on the second pony,' he said. 'Isn't she beautiful?'

His gaze followed the girl on the pony until she, along with the others in the act, made their exit from the ring.

There were a number of other interesting acts—a dare-devil motor-cyclist riding through a ring of fire, the lady-wrestler taking on a rather somnolent bear, and three tigers forming a sort of pyramid atop a revolving platform—but Sitaram was only half-attentive, his thoughts still being with the beautiful, dark, pink-sequinned girl on her white pony.

On the way home he held my hand and sighed.

'I have to go again tomorrow,' he said. 'You'll lend me the money, won't you? I have to see that girl again.'

10

For a couple of weeks Sitaram was busy with the circus, and I did not see much of him. When he wasn't watching the evening performance, he was there in the mornings, hanging round the circus tents, trying to strike up an acquaintance with the ring-hands or minor performers. Most of the artistes and performers were staying in cheap hotels near the railway station. Sitaram appointed himself an unofficial messenger boy, and as he was familiar with every corner of the town, the circus people found him quite useful. He told them where they could get their clothes stitched or repaired, dry-cleaned or laundered; he guided them to the best eating-places, cheap but substantial restaurants such as Komal's or Chacha-da-Hotel (no Indiana or Royal Cafe for the circus crew); posted their letters home; found them barbers and masseurs, brought them newspapers. He was even able to get a copy of the *Madras Mail* for the lady lion-tamer.

Late one night (it must have been after the night show was over) he woke me from a deep dreamless sleep and without any preamble stuffed a laddoo into my mouth. Laddoos were not my favourite sweetmeat, and certainly not in bed at midnight, when the crumbs on the bedsheet were likely to attract an army of ants. While I was still choking on the laddoo, he gave me his good news.

'I've got a job at the circus!'

'What, as assistant to the clown?'

'No, not yet. But the manager likes me. He's made me his office boy. Two hundred rupees a month!'

'Almost as much as I make—but I suppose you'll be running around at all hours. And have you met the girl you liked—the dark girl on the white pony?'

'I have spoken to her. She smiles whenever she sees me. I have spoken to all the girls. They are very nice—especially the ones from the south.'

'Well, you're luckier than I am with girls.'

'Would you like to meet the lady wrestler?'

'The one who wrestles with the bear every night? After that, would she have any time for mere men?'

'They say she's in love with the ringmaster, Mr Victor. He uses his whip if she gets too rough.'

'I don't want to have anything to do with lady wrestlers, lions, bears or whips. Now let me go to sleep. I have to write a story in the morning. Something romantic.'

He leant over and gave me a quick sharp bite on the cheek. I yelped.

'What's that supposed to be?' I demanded.

'An expression of my joy,' he said, and vanished into the night.

The monsoon was only a fortnight away, we were told, and we were all looking forward to some relief from the hot and dusty days of June. Sometimes the nights were even more unbearable, as squadrons of mosquitoes came zooming across the eastern Doon. In those days the eastern Doon was more malarious than the western, probably because it was low-lying in parts and there was more still water in drains and pools. Wild boar and swamp deer abounded.

But it was now mango-time, and this was one of the compensations of summer. I kept a bucket filled with mangoes and dipped into it frequently during the day. So did Anand, Peter, Mohan and others who came by.

One of my more interesting visitors was a writer called G.V. Desani who had, a few years earlier, written a comic novel called *All About H. Hatterr*. I suspect that the character of Hatterr was based on Desani himself, for he was an eccentric individual who told me that he slept in a coffin.

'Do you carry it around with you?' I asked, over a coffee at Indiana.

'No, hotels won't allow me to bring it into the lobby, let alone my room. Hotel managers have a morbid fear of death, haven't they?'

'A coffin should make a good coffee-table. We'll put it to the owner of the Indiana.'

'Trains are fussy too. You can't have it in your compartment, and in the brake-van it gets smashed. Mine's an expensive mahogany coffin, lined with velvet.'

'I wish you many comfortable years sleeping in it. Do you intend being buried in it too?'

'No, I shall be cremated like any other good Hindu. But I may *will* the coffin to a good Christian friend. Would you like it?'

'I rather fancy being cremated myself. I'm not a very successful Christian. A pagan all my life. Maybe I'll get religious when I'm older.'

Mr Desani then told me that he was nominating his own novel for the Nobel Prize, and would I sign a petition that was to be presented to the Nobel Prize Committee extolling the merits of his book? Gladly, I said, always ready to help a good cause. And did I know of any other authors or patrons of literature who might sign? I told him there was Hema Mahajan; and Peter, an eminent Swiss journalist; and old Mrs D'Souza who did a gardening column for *Eve's Weekly*; and Holdsworth at the Doon School—he'd climbed Kamet with Frank Smythe, and had written an account for the journal of the Bombay Natural History Society—and of course there was Anand who was keeping a diary in the manner of Stendhal; and wasn't Mohan planning to write a PhD on P.G. Wodehouse? I gave their names and addresses to the celebrated author, and even added that of the inventor of the Sit-Safe. After all, hadn't he encouraged this young writer by commissioning him to write a brochure for his toilet-seat?

Mr Desani produced his own brochure, with quotes from reviewers and writers who had praised his work. I signed his petition and allowed him to pay for the coffee.

As I walked through the swing doors of the Indiana, Indu and her mother walked in. It was too late for me to turn back. I bowed like the gentleman my grandmother had always wanted me to be, and held the door for them, while they breezed in to the restaurant. Larry Gomes was playing *Smoke Gets In Your Eyes* with a wistful expression.

11

Lady Wart of Worcester, 'Lady Tryiton and the Earl of Stopwater, the Hon. Robin Crazier, Mr and Mrs Paddy Snott-Noble, the Earl and Countess of Lost Marbles, and General Sir Peter de l'Orange-Peel . . .

These were only some of the gracious names that graced the pages of the Doon Club's guest and membership register at the turn of the century, when the town was the favourite retiring place for the English aristocracy. So well did the Club look after its members that most of them remained permanently in Dehra, to be buried in the Chandernagar cemetery just off the Hardwar Road.

In the Dehra cemetery were buried my grandfather, father and a few other relatives. If I sat on their graves, I felt I owned a bit of property. Not a bungalow or even a vegetable patch, but a few feet of well-nourished sod. There were even marigolds flowering at the edges of the graves. And a little blue everlasting that I have always associated with Dehra. It grows in ditches, on vacant plots, in neglected gardens, along footpaths, on the edges of fields, behind lime-kilns, wherever there is a bit of wasteland. Call it a weed if you like, but I have every respect for a plant that will survive the onslaught of brick, cement, petrol fumes, grazing cows and goats, heat and cold (for it flowers almost all the year round), and overflowing sewage. As long as that little flowering weed is still around, there is hope for both man and nature.

A feeling of tranquillity and peace always pervaded my being when I entered the cemetery. Were my long-gone relatives pleased by my presence there? I did not see them in any form, but then, cemeteries are the last place for departed souls to hang around in. Given a chance, they would rather be among the living, near those they cared for or in places where they were happy. I have never been convinced by ghost stories in which the tormented spirit revisits the scene of some ghastly tragedy. Why on earth (or why in heaven) should they want to relive an unpleasant experience?

My grandfather was a man with a mischievous sense of humour who often discomfited his relatives by introducing into their homes odd creatures who refused to go away. Hence the tiny Jharipani bat released into Aunt Mabel's bedroom, or the hedgehog slipped between Uncle Ken's bedsheets. A cousin, Mrs Blanchette, found her house swarming with white rats, while a neighbour received a gift of a parcel of papayas—and in their midst, a bright green and yellow chameleon.

And so, when I was within some fifty to sixty feet of Grandfather's grave, I was not in the least surprised to see a full-grown tiger stretched out on his tombstone apparently enjoying the shade of the magnolia tree which grew beside it.

Was this a manifestation of Timothy (the tiger cub he'd kept when I was a child)? Did the ghosts of long-dead tigers enjoy visiting old haunts? Live tigers certainly did, and when this one stirred, yawned, and twitched its tail, I decided I wouldn't stay to find out if it was a phantom tiger or a real one.

Beating a hasty retreat to the watchman's quarters near the lych-gate, I noticed that a large, well-fed and very real goat was tethered to one of the old tombstones (Colonel Ponsonby of Her Majesty's Dragoons), and I concluded that the tiger had already spotted it and was simply building up an appetite before lunch.

'There's a tiger on Grandfather's grave,' I called out to the watchman, who was checking out his cabbage patch. (And healthy cabbages they were, too.)

The watchman was a bit deaf and assumed that I was complaining about some member of his family, as they were in the habit of grinding their masalas on the smoother gravestones.

'It's that boy Masood,' he said. 'I'll get after him with a stick.' And picking up his lathi, he made for the grave.

A yell, a roar, and the watchman was back and out of the lych-gate before me.

'Send for the police, sahib,' he shouted. 'It's one of the circus tigers. It must have escaped!'

12

Sincerely hoping that Sitaram had not been in the way of the escaping tiger, I made for the circus tents on the parade-ground. There was no show in progress. It was about noon, and everyone appeared to be resting. If a tiger was missing, no one seemed to be aware of it.

'Where's Sitaram?' I asked one of the hands.

'Helping to wash down the ponies,' he replied.

But he wasn't in the pony enclosure. So I made my way to the rear, where there was a cage housing a lion (looking rather sleepy, after its late-night bout with the lady lion-tamer), another cage housing a tiger (looking ready to bite my head off), and another cage with its door open—empty!

Someone came up behind me, whistling cheerfully. It was Sitaram.

'Do you like the tigers?' he asked.

'There's only one here. There are two in the show, aren't there?'

'Of course, I helped feed them this morning.'

'Well, one of them's gone for a walk. Someone must have unlocked the door. If it's the same tiger I saw in the cemetery, I think it's looking for another meal—or maybe just dessert!'

Sitaram ran back into the tent, yelling for the trainer and the ringmaster. And then, of course, there was commotion. For no one had noticed the tiger slipping away. It must have made off through the bamboo-grove at the edge of the parade-ground, through the Forest Rangers College (well-wooded then), circled the police lines and entered the cemetery. By now it could have been anywhere.

It was, in fact, walking right down the middle of Dehra's main road, causing the first hold-up in traffic since Pandit Nehru's last visit to the town. Mr Nehru would have fancied the notion; he was keen on tigers. But the citizens of Dehra took no chances. They scattered at the noble beast's approach. The Delhi bus came to a grinding halt, while tonga-ponies, never known to move faster than a brisk trot, broke into a gallop that would have done them proud at the Bangalore Races.

The only creature that failed to move was a large bull (the one that sometimes blocked the approach to my steps) sitting in the middle of the road, forming a traffic island of its own. It did not move for cars, buses, tongas and trucks. Why budge for a mere tiger?

And the tiger, having been fed on butcher's meat for most of its life, now disdained the living thing

(since the bull refused to be stalked) and headed instead for the back entrance to the Indiana's kitchens.

There was a general exodus from the Indiana. Peter, who had been regaling his friends with tales of his exploits in the Foreign Legion, did not hang around either; he made for the comparative safety of my flat. Larry Gomes stopped in the middle of playing the *Anniversary Waltz*, and fox-trotted out of the restaurant. The owner of the Indiana rushed into the street and collided with the owner of the Royal Cafe. Both swore at each other in choice Pashtu—they were originally from Peshawar. Swami Aiyar, a Doon School boy with ambitions of being a newspaper correspondent, buttonholed me near my landlady's shop and asked me if I knew Jim Corbett's telephone number in Haldwani.

'But he only shoots man-eaters,' I protested.

'Well, they're saying three people have already been eaten in the bazaar.'

'Ridiculous. No self-respecting tiger would go for a three-course meal.'

'All the same, people are in danger.'

'So, we'll send for Jim Corbett. Aurora of the Green Bookshop should have his number.'

Mr Aurora was better informed than either of us. He told us that Jim Corbett had settled in Kenya several years ago.

Swami looked dismayed. 'I thought he loved India so much that he refused to leave.'

'You're confusing him with Jack Gibson of the Mayo School,' I said.

At this point the tiger came through the swing doors of the Indiana and started crossing the road. Mohan was driving slowly down Rajpur Road in his 1936 Hillman. He'd been up half the night, drinking and playing cards, and he had a terrible hangover. He was now heading for the Royal Cafe, convinced that only a chilled beer could help him recover. When he saw the tiger, his reflexes—never very good—failed him completely, and he drove his car onto the pavement and into the plate-glass window of Bhai Dhian Singh's Wine and Liquor Shop. Mohan looked quite happy among the broken rum bottles. The heady aroma of XXX Rosa Rum, awash on the shopping veranda, was too much for a couple of old topers, who began to mop up the liquor with their handkerchiefs. Mohan would have done the same had he been conscious.

We carried him into the deserted Indiana and sent for Dr Sharma.

'Nothing much wrong with him,' said the doc, 'but he looks anaemic,' and proceeded to give him an injection of vitamin B_{12}. This was Dr Sharma's favourite remedy for anyone who was ailing. He was a great believer in vitamins.

I don't know if the B_{12} did Mohan any good, but the jab of the needle woke him up, and he looked around, blinked up at me, and said, 'Thought I saw a tiger. Could do with a drink, old boy.'

'I'll stand you a beer,' I said. 'But you'll have to pay the bill at Bhai Dhian's. And your car needs repairs.'

'And this injection costs five rupees,' said Dr Sharma.

'Beer is the same price. I'll stand you one too.'

So we settled down in the Indiana and finished several bottles of beer, Dr Sharma expounding all the time on the miracle of Vitamin B_{12}, while Mohan told me that he knew now what it felt like to enter the fourth dimension.

The tiger was soon forgotten, and when I walked back to my room a couple of hours later and found the postman waiting for me with a twenty-five rupee money-order from *Sainik Samachar* (the Armed Forces' weekly magazine), I tipped him five rupees and put the rest aside for a rainy day—which, hopefully, would be the morrow, as monsoon clouds had been advancing from the south.

They say that those with a clear conscience usually sleep well. I have always done a lot of sleeping, especially in the afternoons, and have never been unduly disturbed by pangs of conscience, for I haven't deprived any man of his money, his wife, or his song.

I kicked off my chappals and lay down and allowed my mind to dwell on my favourite Mexican proverb: 'How sweet it is to do nothing, and afterwards to rest!'

I hoped the tiger had found a shady spot for his afternoon siesta. With goodwill towards one and all, I drifted into a deep sleep.

13

A dream crept into my sleep . . . a dream which followed the runaway tiger's progress in Dehra town. The tiger padded silently but purposefully past the Dilaram Bazaar, paying no attention to the screaming and shouting of the little gesticulating creatures who fled at his approach. He'd seen them every night at the circus—all in search of excitement, provided there was no risk attached to it!

Walking down from the other end of the Dilaram Road was a tiger of another sort—sub-inspector Sher ('Tiger') Singh, in charge of the local police outpost. 'Tiger' Singh was feeling on top of the world. His little *thana* was notorious for beating up suspected criminals, and he'd had a satisfying night supervising the third-degree interrogation of three young suspects in a case of theft. None of them had broken down and confessed, but 'Tiger' had the pleasure (and what was it, if not a pleasure, an appeal to his senses?) of kicking one youth senseless, blackening the eyes of another, and fracturing the ankle and shinbone of the third. The damage done, they had been ejected into the street with a warning to keep their noses clean in the future.

These young men could have saved themselves from physical injury had they disbursed a couple of hundred rupees to the sub-inspector and his cohorts, but they were unemployed and without friends of substance; so, beaten and humiliated, they crawled home as best they could. (My dream wasn't far removed from reality. Such a character did exist in Dehra, and was dreaded by one and all. For, 'Tiger' Singh liked the money he sometimes picked up from suspects and the relatives of petty offenders; but many years in the service had brought out the sadistic side to his nature, and now he took a certain pleasure in seeing noses broken and teeth knocked out. He claimed that he could extract teeth without anaesthesia, and would do the job free for those who could not afford dentists' bills. There were no takers.)

In my dream he strutted along the pavement, twirling his moustache with one hand and pulling up his trousers with the other. For he was a well-fed gentleman, whose belly protruded above his belt. He had a constant struggle keeping his trousers, along with his heavy revolver holster, from slipping to the ground. Had he not been in the direct path of the tiger, he would have been ignored. But he chose to stand frozen to the ground, really too terrified to reach for his gun or even hitch up his trousers.

The tiger slapped him to the ground, picked him up by his fat neck, and dragged him into the lantana bushes. Sher Singh let out one despairing cry, which turned into a gurgle as the blood spurted from his throat. (How dreams reflect our most concealed desires!)

This tiger did not eat humans. True, he had almost forgotten how to hunt, but his instincts told him that more succulent repasts could be found in the depths of the forest. And the forest was close at hand, so he abandoned the dead policeman, who would have made a more suitable meal for vultures had not his colleagues come and taken him away. His family received a pension and lived fairly happily ever after.

I opened my eyes. Well, it wasn't such a bad dream, though a bit gruesome perhaps. So much for harbouring goodwill towards everybody. What was noteworthy about my dream however was that neither the tiger nor the S.I. was familiar with the Laws of Karma, or Emerson's Law of Compensation, but they appeared to have been working all the same.

The clouds that had gathered over the foothills finally gave way under their burden of moisture. The first rain of the monsoon descended upon the hills, the valley, the town. In minutes, a two-month layer of dust was washed away from trees, rooftops and pavements. The rain swept across the streets of Dehra, sending people scattering for shelter. Umbrellas unfolded for the first time in months. A gust of wind shook the circus tent. I had gone to the circus ground to meet Sitaram. But he wasn't to be found there, so I stood around a bit, waiting for him. The old lion, scenting the rain on the wind, sat up in its cage and gave a great roar of delight. The ponies shook their manes, an elephant trumpeted.

The rain swept over the railway yards, washing the soot and dust from the carriages and engines. It brought freshness and new life to the tea-gardens and sugarcane fields. Even earthworms responded to the cool dampening of their environment and stretched sensuously in the soft mud.

Mud! Buffaloes wallowed in it; children romped in it; frogs broke into antiphonal chants. Glorious, squelchy mud. Hateful for the rest of the year, but wonderfully inviting on the first day of the monsoon. A large amount got washed down from the loose eroded soil of the foothills, so that the streams and canals were soon clogged, silted up, and flooded their banks.

The mango and litchee trees were washed clean. Sal and shisham shook in the wind. Peepal leaves danced. The roots of the banyan drank up the good rain. The neem gave out its heady fragrance. Squirrels ran for shelter into the embracing branches of Krishna's buttercup. Parrots made merry in the guava groves.

I walked home through the rain. Home, did I say? Yes, my small flat was becoming a home, what with Sitaram and his geraniums upstairs, my landlady below, and other familiars in the neighbourhood. Even the geckos on the wall were now recognizable, each acquiring an identity and personality of its own. Sitaram had trained one of them to take food from his fingers. At first he had stuck a bit of meat at the end of a long thin stick. The lizard had snapped up this morsel. Then, every day, he had shortened the stick until the lizard, growing in confidence, took his snack from the short end of the stick and finally from the boy's fingers. I hadn't got around to feeding the wall lizards. One of them had fallen with a plop on my forehead in the middle of the night, and my landlady told me of how a whole family had been poisoned when a gecko had fallen into a cooking pot and been served up with a mixed vegetable curry.

A neighbour, who worked for Madras Coffee House, told me that down south there were a number of omens connected with the fall of the wall lizard, especially if it dropped on some part of your body. He told me that I'd been fortunate that the lizard fell on my forehead, but had it fallen on my tummy I'd have been in for a period of bad luck. But I wasn't taking any chances. The lizards could have all the snacks they wanted from Sitaram, but I wasn't going to encourage any familiarity.

Now, happy to get my clothes wet with the first monsoon shower, I ran up the steps to my room, but found it empty. Then Sitaram's voice, raised in song, wafted down to me from the rooftop. I climbed up to the roof by means of an old iron ladder that was always fixed there, and found him on the flat roof, prancing about in his underwear.

'Come and join me,' he shouted. 'It is good to dance in the first monsoon shower.'

'You might be seen from the roofs across the road,' I said.

'Never mind. Don't you think I look like a hero?'

'Far from it,' I said, and retreated below.

14

It was still 1955, and the middle of the monsoon, when Sitaram decided to throw his lot in with the circus and leave Dehra. Those roses of the south had a lot to do with it. I wasn't sure if he was in love with one of the pony-riders, or with the girl on the flying trapeze.

Perhaps both of them; perhaps all of them. He was at an age when his romantic dreams had to be directed somewhere, and those beautiful dusky circus girls were certainly more approachable, and more glamorous, than the coy college girls we saw every day.

'So you're going to desert me,' I said, when he told me of his plans.

'Only for a few months. I'll see the country this way.'

'Once with the circus, always with the circus.'

'Well, you have your Indu.'

'I don't. I hear she's getting engaged to that cricket-playing princeling. I hate all cricketers!'

'You're better-looking.'

'But I'm not a prince. I haven't any money, and I don't play cricket. Well, I played a little at school, but they always made me twelfth man, which meant carrying out the drinks like a waiter. What a stupid game!'

'I agree. Football is better.'

'More manly. But not as glamorous.'

Sitaram pondered a while, and then gave me the benefit of his wisdom.

'To win Indu you must win her mother.'

'And how do I do that? She's a dragon.'

'Well, you must pretend you like dragons.'

I was sitting in the Indiana, having my coffee, when Indu's mother walked in. She was alone. (Indu was probably with her prince, learning to bowl under-arm). I said good morning and asked her if she'd like to join me for a cup of coffee. To my surprise, she assented. Larry Gomes was playing *Love Is a Many-Splendoured Thing*, and the Maharani was just a bit dreamy-eyed and probably a little sloshed too. But she wasn't in any way attractive. Her eyes were baggy and her skin was coarse (too many skin lotions?) and her chin was developing a dewlap. Would Indu look like her one day?

She drank her coffee and asked me if I would like a drive. On the assumption that she would be driving me to her house, I thanked her and followed her out of the restaurant, while Larry Gomes looked anxiously at me over his spectacles and broke into the *Funeral March*.

15

Well, it was very nearly my funeral.

The Maharani's intentions weren't clear to me before we left the restaurant, but now I couldn't help suddenly noticing the striking similarity between her and the repulsive crocodile. So, how could a monster like the Maharani have produced a beautiful, tender, vivacious, electrifying girl like Indu? It was like making a succulent dish from a pumpkin, a bitter gourd, and a spent cucumber.

The Maharani had denied me the dish, but it looked as if she was prepared to give me the ingredients.

She drove me to her home in her smart little Sunbeam-Talbot, and no sooner was I settled on her sofa, with a glass of Carew's Gin in my hand, than I found my free hand encased in a fold of crocodile skin—her hand!

It had never occured to me that this badly-preserved Christmas pudding could be of an amorous disposition. I had always thought of middle-aged mothers as having gone beyond the pursuit of carnal pleasures. But not this one!

She tried to set me at my ease.

'I'm a child psychologist, you know.'

'But I'm twenty-five.'

'All the better to *treat* you, my dear.'

'Your Highness,' I began.

'Don't "Highness" me, darling. My pet name is Liz.'

'As in lizard?'

'Cheeky! After Queen Elizabeth.' And she gave me a sharp pinch on the thigh. 'You write poetry, don't you? Recite one of your poems.'

'You need moonlight and roses.'

'I prefer sunshine and cactii.'

'Well, here's a funny one.' I was anxious to please her without succumbing to her blandishments and advances. So I recited my latest limerick.

There was a fat man in Lucknow
Who swallowed six plates of pillau,
When his belly went bust
(As distended, it must)
His buttons rained down upon Mhow.

She clapped her hands and shrieked with delight. 'Buttons, buttons!' I then tried to get up from the sofa, but she pulled me down again.

'You deserve a reward,' she said, producing a lump of barley sugar from a box on the side-table. 'This came all the way from Calcutta. Open your mouth.'

Dutifully I opened my mouth. But instead of popping the sweet in, she kissed me passionately.

What can you do in such a situation? Not much, really. You must let the more active partner take over—in this case, the rich Maharani of Magador. She certainly knew how to get you worked up. One thing led to another and the undesirable (as far as I was concerned) but inevitable thing happened.

Afterwards I was rewarded with more barley-sugar and Turkish coffee.

She offered to drop me home, but I said I'd walk. I wanted to put my head in order. My thoughts were in a whirl. How could I be the Maharani's lover while I was in love with her daughter? Love lyrics for Indu, and limericks for her mother?

'There's no justice anywhere,' I said aloud, in my best William Brown manner. "Tisn't fair.' And then, as Popeye would have said, 'It's disgustipating!'

And as I closed the gate and stepped onto the sidewalk, who should appear but Indu, riding pillion on her cricketing prince's Triumph motor-bike. At the sight of him my feelings of guilt evaporated. And looking at Indu, smiling insincerely at me, I began to see points of resemblance between her and her mother. Would she be like the Maharani in twenty years' time? I had never seen her father (the late deceased Maharaja of Magador) but fervently hoped that he had been as goodlooking as his portraits suggested and that Indu had taken after him.

I gave her and her escort a polite bow (after all, why reveal my mind) and set off at a dignified pace in the direction of the bazaar. A car would never be mine, but at least my legs wouldn't atrophy from disuse. Hadn't this very cricketing legend suffered from several torn ligaments in the course of his short career? Chasing cricket balls is a certain way to get a hernia, I said to myself, and then turned my thoughts to the composition of a new limerick in honour of the lady who had just tormented me into becoming her lover. There was no Amnesty International in those days; I had to defend myself in my own way. So I composed the following lines:

They called her the Queen of the Nile,
For she walked like a fat crocodile.
But she said, 'You young boy,
Don't act so coy,'
And took me to bed with a smile.

16

We all need one friend in whom to confide—to whom
we can confess our misdemeanours, look for sympathy
in times of trouble. Sitaram was my only intimate,
and he listened with bated breath while I gave him a
hair-raising account of my experience with the
Maharani. But he wasn't sympathetic. His first response
was the following succinct remark:

'Congratulations, you have signed your own death
warrant.'

'Why?' I asked.

'Because you cannot escape her now. She'll suck
you dry.'

'A succubus, forsooth!'

'Don't use fancy language—you know what I mean.
When an older woman gets hold of a young man, she
doesn't let him go until he's quite useless to her or
anyone else! You'd better join the circus with me.'

'And what do I do in the circus? Feed the animals?'

'They need someone for giving massage.'

'I've always fancied myself as a masseur. Whom do

I get to massage—the acrobats, the dancing-girls, the trapeze artistes?'

'The elephants. They lie down and you massage their legs. And backsides.'

'I'll stick to the Maharani,' I said. 'Her skin has the same sort of texture, but there's not so much of it.'

'Well, please yourself . . . See, I've brought you a pretty tree. Will you look after it while I'm away?'

It was a red oleander in a pot. It was just coming into flower. We placed it on the balcony beside the rose bush and the geraniums. There were several geraniums now—white, cerise, salmon-pink and bright red—and they were all in flower, making quite a display on the sunny veranda.

'I'll look after them,' I said. 'As long as the landlady doesn't turn me out. The rent is overdue.'

'Don't lend money to your friends. Especially that Swiss fellow. He owes money everywhere—hasn't even paid my parents for two months' washing. One of these days he'll just go away—and your money will go with him. There is nothing to keep him here.'

'There is nothing to keep *me* here.'

'This is where you belong, where you grew up. You will always be here.'

It was where I had grown up—my grandparents' home—but I had always been happier with my father, sharing a wartime tent with him on the outskirts of Delhi, visiting the ruins of Old Delhi—Humayun's Tomb, the Purana Killa, the Kashmiri Gate; going to the cinema with him to see the beautiful skating legend, Sonja Henie in *Sun Valley Serenade*; Nelson Eddy singing *Volga Boatmen* and *Ride, Cossack, Ride* in *Balalaika*; Carmen Miranda swinging her hips *Down Argentine Way*; and Hope and Crosby *On the Road to Zanzibar* or *Morocco* or *Singapore*. Rickshaw-rides in Simla. Ice-creams at Davico's. Comics—*Film Fun* and *Hotspur* . . . And those colourful postcards he used to send me once a week. At school, the distribution of the post was always something to look forward to.

But I must also have inherited a great deal of my mother's sensuality, her unconventional attitude to life, her stubborn insistence on doing things that respectable people did not approve of . . . She was a convivial character, who mingled with all and shocked not a few.

I'm sure my mother was quite a handful for my poor father, bookish and intellectual, who did so want her to be a 'lady'. But this was something that went against her nature. She liked to drink and swear a bit. The ladies of the Dehra Benevolent Society had not approved. Nor had they approved of my mother going to church without a hat! This was considered the height of irreverence in those days. There were remonstrances and anguished letters of protest from other (always female) members of the congregation. I wasn't big enough to understand much of all this then—I was only about three years old. My parents separated a year later, so whatever I know is from hearsay.

17

The circus tents were being dismantled and the parade ground was comparatively silent again. Some boys kicked a football around. Others flew kites. The monsoon season is kite-flying time, for it's not too windy, and the moist air-currents are just right for keeping a kite aloft.

In the old part of the Dhamawalla bazaar, there used to be a kite-shop, and, taking a circuitous way home, I stopped at the shop and bought a large pink kite. I thought Sitaram would enjoy flying it from the rooftop when he wasn't dancing in the rain. But when I got home, I found he had gone. His parents told me he had left in a hurry, as most of the circus people had taken the afternoon train to Amritsar. He had taken his clothes and a cracked bathroom mirror, nothing else, and yet the flat seemed strangely empty and forlorn without him. The plants on the balcony were poignant reminders of his presence.

I thought of giving the kite to my landlady's son,

but I knew him to be a destructive brat who'd put his fist through it at the first opportunity, so I hung it on a nail on the bedroom wall, and thought it looked rather splendid there, better than a Picasso although perhaps not in the same class as one of Anand's angels.

As I stood back, admiring it, there was a loud knocking at my door (as in the knocking at the gate in *Macbeth*, portending deeds of darkness) and I turned to open it, wondering why I had bothered to close it in the first place (I seldom did), when something about the knocking—its tone, its texture—made me hesitate.

There are knocks of all kinds—hesitant knocks, confident knocks, friendly knocks, good-news knocks, bad-news knocks, tax-collector's knocks (exultant, these!), policemen's knocks (peremptory, business-like), drunkard's knocks (slow and deliberate), the landlady's knock (you could tell she owned the place) and children's knocks (loud thumps halfway down the door).

I had come to recognize different kinds of knocks, but this one was unfamiliar. It was a possessive kind of knock, gloating, sensual, bold and arrogant. I stood a chair on a table, then balanced myself on the chair and peered down through the half-open skylight.

It was Indu's mother. Her perfume nearly knocked me off the chair. Her bosom heaved with passion and expectancy, her eyes glinted like a hyena's and her crocodile hands were encased in white gloves!

I withdrew quietly and tiptoed back across the room and out on the balcony. On the next balcony, my neighbour's maidservant was hanging out some washing.

'For God's sake,' I told her. 'That woman out front, banging on my door. Go and tell her I'm not at home!'

'Who is she?'

'A *rakshasi*, if you want to know.'

'Then I'm not going near her!'

'All right, can you let me out through your flat? Is there anyone at home?'

'No, but come quickly. Can you climb over the partition?'

The partition did not look as if it would take my weight, so I climbed over the balcony wall and, clinging to it, moved slowly along the ledge till I got to my neighbour's balcony. The maidservant helped me over. Such nice hands she had! How could a working girl have such lovely hands while a lady of royal lineage had crocodile-skin hands? It was the law of compensation, I suppose; Mother Nature looking after her own.

'What's your name?' I whispered, as she led me through her employer's flat and out to the back stairs.

'Radha,' she said, her smile lighting up the gloom.

'Rather you than that *rakshasi* outside!' I gave her hand a squeeze and said, 'I'll see you again,' then took off down the stairs as though a swarm of bees was after me.

My landlady's son's bicycle was standing in the veranda. I decided to borrow it for a couple of hours.

I rode vigorously until I was out of the town, and then I took a narrow unmetalled road through the sal forest on the Hardwar road. I thought I would be safe there, but it wasn't long before I heard the menacing purr of the Maharani's Sunbeam-Talbot. Looking over my shoulder, I saw it bumping along in a cloud of dust. It was like a chase-scene in a Hitchcock film, and I was Cary Grant about to be machine-gunned from a low-flying aircraft. I saw another narrow trail to the right, and swerved off the road, only to find myself parting company with the bicycle and somersaulting into some lantana bushes. There was a screech of brakes, a car door shot open, and the rich Maharani of Magador was bounding towards me like a man-eating tigress.

'Jim Corbett, where are you?' I called feebly.

'He has no business here, you fool,' said the tigress. Once again I lost out to the grim determination of the Maharani . . . Was there going to be no respite from her?

18

A change of air was needed. What with the attentions of the Maharani, the borrowings of Peter, the loss of Indu, and the absence of Sitaram, I wasn't doing much writing. My bank balance was very low. I had also developed a throat infection (don't ask me how).

There was a sum of two hundred and seventy rupees in the bank. Always prudent, I withdrew two hundred and fifty and left twenty rupees for my last supper. Then I packed a bag, and left my keys with the landlady with the entreaty that she tell no one in Dehra of my whereabouts, and took the bus to Rishikesh.

Rishikesh was then little more than a village, scattered along the banks of the Ganga where it cut through the foothills. There were a few ashrams and temples, a tiny bazaar, and a police outpost. The saffron-robed sadhus and ascetics outnumbered the rest of the population. I couldn't help remembering that trip to Rishikesh my friend Sudheer and I had undertaken . . . Sudheer had wanted to avoid being caught by the police, so he had disguised himself as a sadhu. But surely, he couldn't be hanging around here now—he was always a rolling stone.

There had been a break in the rains, and I spent a night sleeping on the sands sloping down to the river.

The next night it did rain, and I moved to a bench on the small railway platform. I could have stayed in one of the two ashrams, but I had no pretensions to religion of any kind, and was not inclined to become an acolyte to some holy man. Kim had his Lama, the braying Beatles had their Master, and others have had their gurus and godmen, but I have always been stubborn and thick-headed enough to want to remain my own man—myself, warts and all, singing my own song. Nobody's *chela*, nobody's camp-follower.

Let nature reign, let freedom sing! . . .

And, so, on the third morning of my voluntary exile from the fleshpots of Dehra, I strode up the river, taking a well-worn path which led to the shrines in the higher mountains. I was not seeking salvation or enlightenment; I wished merely to come to terms with myself and my situation.

Should I stay on in Dehra, or should I strike out for richer pastures—Delhi or Bombay perhaps? Or should I return to London and my desk in the Photax office? Oh, for the life of a clerk! Or I could give English tuitions, I supposed. Except that everyone seemed to know English. What about French? I'd picked up a French patois in the Channel Islands. It wasn't the real thing, but who would know the difference?

I practised a few lines, reciting aloud to myself:

Jeune femme au rendezvous.
(She is waiting for her lover.)
Oh, oui! Il va venir
(Oh, yes, he is coming!)
Enfin je le verra!
(Finally I shall see him!)
Pourquoi je attends?
(What am I waiting for?)

I could see my flat overflowing with students from all over Dehra and beyond. But how was I to keep the Maharani from attending?

The future looked rather empty as I trudged forlornly up the mountain trail. What I really needed just then was a good companion—someone to confide in, someone with whom to share life's little problems. No wonder people get married! An admirable institution, marriage. But who'd marry an indigent writer, with twenty rupees in the bank and no prospects in a land where English was on the way out. (I was not to know that English would be 'in' again, thirty years later.) No self-respecting girl really wants to share the proverbial attic with a down-and-out writer; least of all the princess Indu from Magador.

I should have taken my cricket more seriously, I told myself. Must dress better. Put on the old school tie.

But did I really, really want to be bogged down by marriage? Even if it might be with Indu? Sure, married life had several admirable qualities, but did it not mean sacrifice, adjustment and so many other selfless things? Could I truly balance my first priority—of being a full-fledged writer—with the responsibilities of a married man? I wasn't so sure . . . I wanted to lead a fairly unfettered life so that I could focus entirely and solely on my writing. All I needed and wanted was a room of my own, my own space, and my simple needs to be met. A room of my own . . . yes, that had been my dream many years ago as well, long before I had the room on the roof of the Kapoors' house. When had I discovered that this was my dream? That day—when an old man, a beggar man bent double, with a flowing white beard and piercing grey eyes, stopped on the road on the other side of the garden wall and looked up at me, where I perched on the branch of a lichee tree. I was staying with my grandmother at her house then—in Dehra.

'What's your dream?' he asked.

It was a startling question coming from that raggedy old man on the street. Even more startling that it should have been asked in English. English-speaking beggars were a rarity in those days.

'What's your dream?' he repeated.

'I don't remember,' I said. 'I don't think I had a dream last night.'

'That's not what I mean. You know it isn't what I mean. I can see you're a dreamer. It's not the lichee season, but you sit in that tree all afternoon, dreaming.'

'I just like sitting here,' I said. I refused to admit that I was a dreamer. Other boys didn't dream, they had catapults.

'A dream, my boy, is what you want most in life. Isn't there something that you want more than anything else?'

'Yes,' I said promptly. 'A room of my own.'

'Ah! A room of your own, a tree of your own, it's the same thing. Not many people can have their own rooms, you know. Not in a land as crowded as ours.'

'Just a small room.'

'And what kind of room do you live in at present?'

'It's a big room, but I have to share it with my Uncle Ken and even my aunts if there are too many of us at the same time.'

'I see. What you really want is freedom. Your own tree, your own room, your own small place in the sun.'

'Yes, that's all.'

'That's all? That's everything! When you have all that, you'll have found your dream.'

'Tell me how to find it!'

'There's no magic formula, my friend. If I was a godman, would I be wasting my time here with you?

You must work for your dream and move towards it all the time, and discard all those things that come in the way of finding it. And then, if you don't expect too much too quickly, you'll find your freedom, a room of your own. The difficult time comes afterwards.'

'Afterwards?'

'Yes, because it's so easy to lose it all, to let someone take it away from you. Or you become greedy, or careless, and start taking everything for granted, and—poof!—suddenly the dream has gone, vanished!'

'How do you know all this?' I asked.

'Because I had my dream and lost it.'

'Did you lose everything?'

'Yes, just look at me now, my friend. Do I look like a king or a godman? I had everything I wanted, but then I wanted more and more . . . . You get your room, and then you want a building, and when you have your building you want your own territory, and when you have your own territory you want your own kingdom—and all the time it's getting harder to keep everything. And when you lose it—in the end, all kingdoms are lost—you don't even have your room any more.'

'Did you have a kingdom?'

'Something like that . . . . Follow your own

dream, boy, but don't take other people's dreams, don't stand in anyone's way, don't take from another man his room or his faith or his song.' And he turned and shuffled away, intoning the following verse which I have never heard elsewhere, so it must have been his own—

Live long, my friend, be wise and strong,
But do not take from any man his song.

These memories in mind, I found myself standing on the middle of a small wooden bridge in Rishikesh that crossed one of the swift mountain streams that fed the great river. No, I wasn't thinking of hurling myself on the rocks below. The thought would have terrified me! I'm the sort who clings to life no matter how strong the temptation is to leave it. But absent-mindedly I leant against the wooden railing of the bridge. The wood was rotten and gave way immediately.

I fell some thirty feet, fortunately into the middle of the stream where the water was fairly deep. I did not strike any rocks. But the current was swift and carried me along with it. I could swim a little (thank God for those two years in the Channel Islands), and as I'd lost my chappals in my fall, I swam and drifted with the current, even though my clothes were an encumbrance. The breast-stroke seemed the best in those turbulent waters, but ahead I saw a greater turbulence and knew I was approaching rapids and, possibly, a waterfall. That would have spelt the end of a promising young writer.

So I tried desperately to reach the river bank on my right. I got my hands on a smooth rock but was pulled away by the current. Then I clutched at the branch of a dead tree that had fallen into the stream. I held fast; but I did not have the strength to pull myself out of the water.

Looking up I saw my father standing on the grassy bank. He was smiling at me in the way he had done that lazy afternoon at the canal. Was he beckoning to me to join him in the next world, or urging me to make a bid to continue for a while in this one?

I made a special effort—yes, I was a stout-hearted young man then—heaved myself out of the water and climbed along the waterlogged tree-trunk until I sank into ferns and soft grass.

I looked up again, but the vision had gone. The air was scented with wild roses and magnolia.

You may break, you may shatter
the vase if you will,
But the scent of the roses will linger
there still.

19

Back to sleepy Dehra, somnolent in the hot afternoon sun and humid from the recent rain. Dragonflies hovered over the canals. Mosquitoes bred in still waters, multiplying their own species and putting a brake on ours. Someone at the bus stand told me that the Maharani was down with malaria; as a result I walked through the bazaar with a spring in my step, even though my cheap new chappals were cutting into the flesh between my toes. Underfoot, the neem-pods gave out their refreshing though pungent odour. This was home, even though it did not offer fame or riches.

As I approached Astley Hall, I saw a pink kite flying from the roof of my flat. The landlady's son had probably got hold of it. It darted about, pirouetted, made extravagant nose-dives, recovered and went through teasing little acrobatic sallies, as though it had a life of its own. A pink kite against a turquoise-blue sky.

It was definitely my kite. How dare my landlady presume I had no need for it! I hurried to the stairs, stepping into cowdung as I went, and consoling myself with the thought that stepping into fresh cowdung was considered lucky, at least according to Sitaram's mother.

And perhaps it was, because, as I took the narrow

stairway to the flat roof, who should I find up there but Sitaram himself, flying my kite without a care in the world.

When he saw me, he tied the kite-string to a chimney-stack and ran up and gave me a tight hug. 'Why aren't you with the circus?' I asked.

'Left the circus,' he said, and we sat down on the parapet and exchanged news.

'What made you leave so suddenly? You were ready to follow those circus-girls wherever they went.'

'They are all in Ambala. There's a big parade-ground there. But it was too hot. Much hotter than Dehra.'

'Is that why you left—because of the heat?'

'Well, there was also this tiger that escaped.'

'But it escaped in Dehra! Don't tell me it returned to the circus?'

'No, no! This was the other tiger. It got out of its cage, somehow.'

'Not again! Did *you* have anything to do with it?'

'Of course not. I hadn't been near it since early that morning.'

'Someone must have left the cage open. Or failed to close it properly.'

'Must have been Mr Victor, the ringmaster. Anyway, when he tried to drive it back into the cage, it sprang on him and took his arm off. He's in hospital.'

'And the tiger?'

'It ran into the sugarcane fields. No one saw it again.'

'So the circus has lost both its tigers and the ringmaster his arm. Has the lion escaped too, since you've been there?'

'No, the lion's too old. Besides, it's deeply in love with the lady-wrestler.'

'I thought that was the dwarf.'

'They both love her.'

I gave up. I had a sneaking suspicion that he'd had something to do with the escape of the tiger, but he managed to convince me that he'd come back (a) because of the heat and (b) because he missed me. In that order. Had it been the other way round, I wouldn't have believed him.

I collected my keys from the landlady (Sitaram had gone into the flat through the skylight), and she gave me a couple of letters. One of them contained a cheque from the *Weekly*, with a note from its editor, saying he would be happy to serialize my next novel. The cheque was for seven hundred rupees.

'We're rich!' I shouted, showing Sitaram the cheque. 'Well, for two or three months, at least . . . See, I told you I'd be a successful writer some day!'

'Will there be more cheques?'

'As long as I keep writing.'

'Then sit down and write.' He pulled a chair up for me and forced me to sit in front of my desk.

'Not now, you ass. I'll start tomorrow.'

'No, *today*!'

And so, to make him happy, I wrote a new limerick:

There was a young fellow called Ram
Who set up a frantic alarm,
For he'd let loose a tiger,
Two bears and a liger,
Who bit off the ringmaster's arm.

'What's a liger?'

'A cross between a lion and a lady-wrestler.'

'Write more about me.'

'Tomorrow. Now let's go out and celebrate.'

We went to one of the sweetshops near the bazaar and ate jalebis. Anand found us there and we ate more jalebis.

Then, walking down Rajpur Road, we met Peter, who said he was badly in need of a drink. So we took him to the Royal Cafe, where we found Mohan funding on the fourth dimension. There were several drinks, and everyone got drunk. Mohan so forgot himself that he signed the chit for the drinks.

It was late evening when we rolled into the Indiana for dinner. Larry Gomes played *Roll out the Barrel* and joined us for a beer.

I couldn't write the next day because I had a terrible hangover. But I started again the following day, and I have been writing ever since.